Last Immortal Dragon

Last Immortal Dragon
ISBN-13: 978-1517644826
ISBN-10: 1517644828
Copyright © 2015, T. S. Joyce
First electronic publication: September 2015

T. S. Joyce
www.tsjoycewrites.wordpress.com

All Rights Are Reserved. No part of this book may be used or reproduced in any manner whatsoever without written permission, except in the case of brief quotations embodied in critical articles and reviews. The unauthorized reproduction or distribution of this copyrighted work is illegal. No part of this book may be scanned, uploaded or distributed via the Internet or any other means, electronic or print, without the author's permission.

NOTE FROM THE AUTHOR:
This book is a work of fiction. The names, characters, places, and incidents are products of the writer's imagination or have been used fictitiously and are not to be construed as real. Any resemblance to persons, living or dead, actual events, locale or organizations is entirely coincidental. The author does not have any control over and does not assume any responsibility for third-party websites or their content.

Published in the United States of America

First digital publication: October 2015
First print publication: October 2015

Last Immortal Dragon

T. S. Joyce

ONE

I'll find you again.

Damon Daye sat straight up in bed and gasped. His lungs burned as if he'd been holding his breath for too long, and deep within his chest, the clicking of his firestarter sounded. Shit. He bolted for the miniature fridge near his bed and threw it open, then chugged two bottled waters without halting.

That's just what he needed—to burn his entire lair down because of one dream. With a shaky sigh, he slid to the floor, back against the cold plastic of the fridge. What in the hell had brought that dream about? He hadn't thought of Feyadine in years.

He squeezed his eyes closed and tried to banish the remnant memories of the dream. It was the one that used to torture him. The one of her final breaths.

"You were screaming," Mason said from the chair in the corner.

Damon startled and stifled the low rumble in his throat. With a sigh, he said, "Careful not to get yourself burned alive, old friend. You shouldn't come in here when I'm slumbering. Not ever."

"Slumbering," Mason repeated with a grin. He did that a lot, repeated the antiquated words Damon sometimes used when he wasn't fully awake yet.

Damon stood, sauntered over to his wall of windows, and hit the switch that retracted the blackout panels. He slept best in rooms that resembled caves. Gray, early morning light streamed under the panels as they lifted, and Damon ran his hands through his disheveled hair. It used to bother him that Mason saw him like this, in the vulnerable moments after waking, but he'd been his assistant and driver for so long now, he trusted him wholly.

"This is your intervention," Mason murmured.

Damon shot him a glare over his shoulder. Mason was sitting in an old velvet chair with his hands clasped over his knees, leaning forward with his eyes blazing the bright blue color of his boar shifter people. Ah. Damon's inner dragon had riled Mason up more than his steady voice let on.

"Intervention for what? I don't host any addictions."

"I've watched you spiral lately. I've kept quiet about it, but you need a change."

Damon clasped his hands behind his back and stared out the window at his mountains. Mason always saw too much of his unrest. He wasn't wrong. Damon had been fighting crippling loneliness, which was only getting worse if that dream was anything to go by. "What kind of change?"

"A mate."

Damon snorted. "Be serious."

"I am. I've never seen you attach to anyone, not in all the years I've served you."

"I've bred females."

"Bred females," Mason repeated.

Damon narrowed his eyes at a flock of birds that lifted from the canopy below his mansion. He really hated when Mason mimicked him.

He slid his driver a dangerous, slit-eyed glare. "Don't mention a mate to me again."

"Fine, then I think it's time for you to raise another child. Male dragons require that, and you haven't raised one since Diem."

"And we both know how good I was at fathering her," he said darkly, regretting all the things he'd done to hurt her. He'd thought he'd been a good father throughout the millennia, but it turned out he'd been shit at nurturing. He'd made strides to mend the fences between he and Diem, and they were good now, but he still harbored deep regrets about her upbringing.

"You could do it differently this time. I see a difference in you. The Ashe Crew and Gray Backs...hell, even Kong has softened you."

"Dragons don't go soft, Mason, and I can't do a mate. Watching her age and die would destroy me. I can't do it again."

"Then we'll track down a breeder. We'll conduct the interviews and sign a contract and you can settle your dragon with offspring. You always do best when you are caring for a female and raising a child. You do."

Another rumble rattled Damon's chest. He didn't like being told when he should cover a woman. That was a choice his dragon made, and right now, his inner monster was freefalling.

Softening? Mason was right, though Damon would never admit it out loud. After centuries of feeling nothing, he'd been letting the bear shifter crews in, little by little. His stony heart was cracking and breaking apart. Tiny earthquakes were busting him up from the middle out because he had grown attached to the shifters in his mountains.

No, allowing anyone else into his life right now was a repulsive idea.

Not until he could find a way to stop feeling again.

****

"Ow," Clara Sutterfield groaned, holding her forehead where the teenager in seat 14B had just whacked her with his carry-on bag.

"My bad," he murmured as he made his way out into the center aisle.

Clara glared. She hated flying. Loathed it. Abhorred everything about it. The lines to get into the airport, the astronomical fees to keep her old Honda in the parking garage, stripping down to her bare essentials at the security checks, that machine that had probably x-rayed her down to her hoo-hah flaps, and she definitely despised the TSA agent who was grinning at her when he picked her out of the crowd to step into the contraption. She was wearing a tank top and cut-off shorts. What could she have possibly been hiding? They'd even dusted her fingers for powder residue.

She got it. She really did. Safety first and all, but she was pretty sure she was picked on because she was a registered shifter.

But none of that—not a bit of it—compared to the actual flying. Her journey had been split up by two brutal layovers, one of which she'd fallen asleep in a chair and had nearly missed her connecting flight.

But she was here, and in one piece, and not a colorful smear on the pavement from a plane crash. Bloody Marys had gotten her through. The teen had probably bopped her on the head on purpose because she had refused to let him syphon off her drink about six times.

Clara smiled politely and gestured a harried mother with an infant in front of her.

"I'm just happy to get off the flight with that crying kid," a man in a business suit muttered behind the mother. "If you can't keep your kid from crying, you should just stay at home with it."

Clara let her pissed-off bear out just enough to glare at the man with a dead, toothy grin and probably bright blue, inhuman eyes. Hey, she was registered, and not having to hide her inner animal was basically the only perk to this gig. She even let off a snarl until the man stepped back from the woman.

"Pardona moi," Clara murmured as she muscled her white, floral duffle bag into the aisle in front of the man-baby. Hadn't he seen the mother pacing the center aisle trying to keep her baby calm? For chrissakes, she'd done everything she could, and could anyone blame the baby for not wanting to be cooped up on the plane with that grumpy butt face? Poor kid couldn't even drink Bloody Marys. "Hi," Clara cooed at the baby, giving a gummy smile over her mother's shoulder. The woman struggled with a bag so Clara offered to help.

"Thank you," the woman said on a relieved breath. "I've never flown with her before." She turned and exclaimed, "Oh!"

Clara scrunched up her nose. "It's the eyes, right? I'm a shifter. They'll fade in a minute."

The woman, bless her, only looked taken aback for a moment before a smile took her face. "I've never met one of you before."

Clara laughed and moved forward behind the woman. The line was brutally slow. "Yeah, I didn't much like being caged on this plane either," she said with a goofy face for the grinning, drooling baby. What a cutie-pie. Big hazel eyes and chubby cheeks and oh! She wanted to cuddle her up. But she wouldn't because that would be weird and she would get arrested.

Out of the plane at last, Clara carried the woman's luggage until she met up with her awaiting husband and didn't need her help anymore. Clara smiled, waved goodbye, and tried her best to ignore the slashing ache through her middle when she ripped her gaze away from that cute little baby. She wanted one of those. She'd wanted a cub of her own since she was twenty, but sometimes things just didn't work out like that.

Okay, she didn't have any luggage other than the carry-on bag on her shoulder, so next up was tracking down a taxi. Or a bus? She looked around the small airport and hoped they had taxi service out in the wilderness. When she'd searched Saratoga online, it looked like a tiny guacamole stain on the map.

"Ms. Sutterfield?" A dark-headed man with animated eyebrows and soft brown eyes held a sign higher. It definitely had her name scribbled across it.

"That's me," she said, confused.

The man stared for a moment too long to be polite. "Uh, I'm Mason." He tucked the sign under his arm and offered his hand, still staring. His attention was flattering, but she knew what she looked like. Frizzy, red hair drawn up in curls thanks to the rainy weather, freckles everywhere, and green eyes not lined with mascara or eyeliner because she thought she would do her make-up in the taxi. Or on the bus.

"You a ginger chaser?" she asked, cocking her head.

"A what?" Mason's eyes widened with comprehension. "Oh, no, you just look familiar."

She drew up short and clutched her bag to her middle. Well, that was new. Her look was...unique. She'd never been mistaken for anyone else in her entire life.

"Can I carry your bag to the car for you, Ms. Sutterfield?"

"Clara, please, and no." She eyed his neatly pressed black suit and cleared her throat, wishing she would've dressed up a bit more. "I mean, no thank you."

Mason was staring again.

Cocking her eyebrow, Clara glared. "I know karate."

"Lie."

"You a shifter?"

Mason nodded once and turned on his heel, then began walking toward a glowing red exit sign.

"Ewey, what kind?"

"It's not polite to ask—"

"Snore, what kind or I'm going to guess." Mason kept on walking, his fists now clenched and swinging at his sides. "Sea cucumber? They look like penises."

Mason gave an amused grunt, but didn't enlighten her. Instead, he said, "You're a lot different than I imagined you."

"Uh, do you often imagine the people you hire before you see them? Don't be a creeper. And while we're on the subject of my hiring, like I told you on the phone, I'm more of a tarot card and palm-reading kind of psychic. I don't know how much help I can be for your ghost problem. I haven't even done a séance. And between you and me, I'm not even that good at telling fortunes."

With a troubled furrow in his brow, Mason popped the trunk of a black, polished Towncar. He settled his hands formally behind his back while she hefted the heavy duffle into the trunk, then he opened her door and waited until she was buckled to walk around the car and slip in behind the wheel.

"And I saw how much my plane ticket cost you. Six hundred bucks! That's not chump change for someone who has mediocre psychic skills and zero background in ghosts."

"Money isn't an issue, so don't worry at all about your travel costs."

"So you're just rolling in the dough."

"I hired you for my boss."

"Wait, I thought I was dealing with you."

"Ms. Sutterfield—"

"Mason, I swear to God I'm going to scream if you keep talking to me like I'm a grandma. I'm thirty, not seventy. Please, call me Clara."

"Thirty," he murmured.

Clara narrowed her eyes at the back of his head and sank into the back seat. The car was spotless and smelled of new leather. Black on black. Nice. Mr. Sea Cucumber's boss had taste.

"I could've hired other psychics, but I want to deal with you. You're a registered shifter, and this is a sensitive…job. Even if you aren't able to do anything for my boss, it will be worth the money"—he pitched his voice low—"just to see the look on his face."

"I can hear you. Bear ears."

"I didn't expect you to be so dominant."

"Why, because I'm a woman?"

"No." He lifted his dark eyes to the rearview mirror and then back to the road in front of him. "Maybe."

Clara rolled her eyes and crossed her arms over her bag. Figured. If she had a penny for every time someone underestimated her on the basis of gender, she could probably pay the late rent on her tarot card business. Clara's Tarot was going under, and fast. She wouldn't have even considered a job like this if Mason, or whoever Mason was working for, hadn't offered her two thousand dollars plus travel expenses just to come out. Sounded too good to be true, but she'd already been paid half upfront, so the job seemed legit enough.

And now her curiosity was piqued about Mason's boss. What kind of trouble were ghosts causing that could make a rich man hire a second-rate palm reader? Sounded like desperation to her. She pitied him already. Ghosts were no joke and could make life miserable. She should know. Her grandmother went mad with the sight. Clara had accepted long ago that her fate would be the same— madness if she couldn't find a way to control the dreams and headaches.

She might not be a great psychic, but she saw things. Awful things that had nothing to do with this world. Teeth and wings and fire, and even though she didn't have a ghost problem, she pitied anyone who was being haunted.

And as the scenery outside her window turned from the cityscape around the Cheyenne Regional Airport to the lush Wyoming evergreen wilderness, she promised herself she would do her best to help Mason and his boss.

TWO

Clara stared up to the towering mansion built into the side of a stark cliff face. The walls were covered in windows, and sleek modern lines said someone had paid an architect a lot of money to design this place. She'd never seen anything like it. To the side of the structure was a waterfall tumbling straight down over the cliff's edge and into a rushing river that snaked off into the forest.

"Whoa," she murmured on a stunned breath.

"Impressed?" Mason asked through an amused smile. He would be very handsome if he didn't ruffle her feathers so easily.

"Your boss is a billionaire, isn't he?"

"Does that bother you?"

"A little. I can't even pay my rent on time, and my body would revolt if I ate anything other than freeze-dried noodle bowls. I'm feeling a little prejudiced right now, but it'll probably pass."

Mason snorted. "Well, at least you're honest. This way."

He snatched her bag out of her hands before she could resist and led her up a winding stone pathway to the front porch. The double doors alone looked as though they belonged to some ancient castle. Scuffed wood, scratched, and stained a deep red color. Giant serpent head door knockers made her want to try one just to see what kind of noise it would make. When she reached for one of the heavy metal knockers, however, Mason gave her a grumpy look, so she clenched her hand and abstained.

Mason hesitated in the sprawling, white marble entryway. "Whatever happens now," he whispered, "I'd ask that you refrain from sharing what you experience here."

What the hell kind of ghosts required secrecy? She held up three fingers and swore, "Werebear's honor."

Mason didn't look amused. "Follow me."

Why was he whispering like this place was a library and not a modern day fortress. Her flip flops clacked loudly across the slippery marble floors, and she cleared her throat nervously. "I thought I would have a chance to change my clothes before I got here."

Mason didn't answer.

"I would've worn a dress..." She sidled away from a statue of a Grecian man with a water fountain coming out of his tiny penis and splashing into a marble bowl below him. "Or something."

"Lie."

Gah, he was so annoying. "Perhaps dresses aren't my thing, but I would've worn pants." Probably. She tugged at the short hem of her cutoff shorts and pulled up the scoop neck of her tank top to cover her cleavage a little better. "These are my traveling clothes." Another lie but Mason didn't point it out. She lived on the coast of Florida, and beachwear was all the rage. "Or a shirt with sleeves." Because this one was definitely not covering the dragon tattoo she had on her shoulder. And was that an actual metal suit of arms? "It feels like Antarctica in here."

"Do you ever stop talking?"

Clara stifled the urge to trip him by his polished shoes, but just barely. "Not when I'm nervous."

"A dominant grizzly like yourself?

Nervous? I don't believe that."

"I've never met a sea cucumber shifter before. You intimidate me, Mason."

The dark-haired man shook his head in annoyance, but didn't respond. This place felt like a mausoleum, and not only that, but there was a weight here she didn't understand. And the deeper she followed Mason into the home, the more it pressed upon her shoulders and made it hard to breathe. Maybe it was because she was traveling deeper into the side of the cliff. Even with a bear inside of her, she'd never been a fan of caves or tight places.

Mason reached a set of twenty-foot tall mahogany double doors and inhaled deeply before he pushed them open. Not wanting to be left alone, Clara looked back down the long, cold corridor from which they'd come and scurried in after Mason.

"Mr. Daye, I'd like to introduce you to Ms. Clara Sutterfield."

Clara locked eyes on the man behind the desk and jerked to a stop. His raven-black hair was short on the sides and longer on top. Right at his temples, he'd gone slightly silver, but his maturity there didn't match his smooth, wrinkle-less face. His sharp jaw clenched, and a muscle twitched there. His eyes went from the color of pitch to the silver of a knife blade in an instant. A spark of recognition in his gaze matched hers, though she couldn't put her finger on where she'd seen him before.

He sat there behind the desk with a stack of papers in front of him and his pen tip resting on one like he'd been in the middle of signing. She couldn't breathe. Couldn't draw a single breath trapped in his gaze like this, and the hairs on the back of her neck lifted. A soft rumble filled the room, but it wasn't the growl of a fellow grizzly. He was something bigger. Only something truly terrifying would make a warning sound like that. Inside, her bear screamed to run—run away from this place and never look back.

The man blinked slowly, and his pupils dilated and lengthened in that churning silver color to look like a snake's. Holy shit. He was beautiful. Lethal, deadly, but with an angelic face.

When the man ripped his gaze away from her, she stumbled backward and gasped air. Mason was watching her with a confused expression, but dragged his attention to Mr. Daye as she took another step back. Her shoulder blades hit the wall, and she clenched her hands against the urge to flee.

She knew this man. Right? She knew him from somewhere. The first shooting pain of one of her debilitating headaches slashed through her mind, making her wince.

"Damon," Mason said low.

"Damon," she whispered. Something about that name…

The man's reptilian eyes tightened, and he stood slowly, arms locked on the desk, muscles flexing against his white oxford shirt. "Please tell me she's not who I think she is."

All around him, the air wavered and darkened. Three shadows, no four, stood behind his desk, about the same height as Mr. Daye. She couldn't tell if the apparitions were men or women. Only that he was, in fact, being haunted. The veil that stood between this world and the next made them look like nothing more than gray mist.

"You have," she said, pointing a shaking finger, "g-g-g…" She tried again, digging deep to find her bravery that seemed to have left the freaking building. "You have…"

Mr. Daye gritted his teeth and leveled her with a brutal glare. "Spit it out."

"G-g-ghosts."

Damon looked behind him with a slit-eyed glare, and the rumble in his chest grew stronger. Now, the terrifying sound vibrated off her skin and made her wish she could disappear into the wall.

When he returned his inhuman gaze to her, he said, "Tell me, Mrs. Sutterfield. What is your occupation?"

This was usually where she embellished to hook customers, but with Mr. Daye, she couldn't seem to fib. "I'm a shite psychic. Tarot cards and palm readings. And apparently ghosts, as of just now. I'm not very good. Terrible at it, in fact."

"A psychic?"

"Mmm hmmm."

"A seer?" Mr. Daye dragged his pissed attention to Mason, who had the good sense to be cowering against the other wall right along with her.

Mason dipped his chin once, his lightened gaze on the carpet. "She is of Feyadine's line, ancestor to her brother, Nall, and a grizzly shifter."

Mr. Daye's eyes tightened at the corners as he sat slowly into his chair. "Leave us."

Okie dokie then. Clara went to high-knee her ass out of the office, but Mason beat her to the door. "I'm sorry," he whispered, looking regretful as he pulled the door closed. From the other side, the click of a lock sound. She gave the handles a stout yank to no avail. "Son of mother-fluffin'—"

"Ms. Sutterfield, please have a seat."

"Polite decline," she said in a mousey voice, afraid to turn around and face him. His furious expression was so much worse than the ghosts standing patiently behind him.

"I won't hurt you."

She exhaled a shaky breath and turned around with her eyes squeezed closed. When she popped one open, Mr. Daye was studying her with his head cocked and a frown marring his features.

Somehow he'd grown even more handsome in the time she'd tried to escape.

"Do you know why Mason has brought you here?"

"To exorcise your ghosts?" *Please lawd, let it not be to serve as dinner for this monster shifter.*

"I'm afraid not. Apparitions don't bother men like me."

She pointed. "There's one right there and another right there—"

"Didn't say they weren't there, Ms. Sutterfield. Only that they don't bother me."

"Are they people you've…"

Damon's eyes narrowed to slits. "People I've what? Say what's on your mind."

"Are they people you've killed?"

Damon cast another quick glance over his shoulder, then rested his elbows on the desk and clasped his hands in front of his mouth. With a challenging look in his eyes, he smiled coldly and said, "Perhaps."

She cleared her throat so her voice wouldn't come out all pitchy and terrified. "You don't have to call me Ms. Sutterfield. Please call me Clara." Yes, that's right. Make him realize she was an actual person and maybe he wouldn't serial kill her.

"Clara, you can call me Damon. Now, please have a seat."

She crossed her arms and lifted her chin. "Thank you, Damon, but I'd rather stand." Over here where the man couldn't reach her.

He angled his head, never taking those bright silver eyes from her. "As you wish." He sighed and pulled a stapled stack of paperwork from a drawer in his sprawling desk. "Mason brought you here to see if you would be agreeable to breeding with me."

Clara's mouth flopped open. "Say what now?"

"I would pay you a substantial amount of

money in return for bearing my offspring."

"Sex?" Really? That was the only word she could push past her tightening vocal chords right now?

"No sex. I like it less personal than that. We would let the doctors help us get you pregnant."

"Less personal. Right." She was floating. With a frown, she looked down at her neon pink flip flops, but nope, they were still embedded in the thick carpet. "This looks expensive."

"The carpet?"

"Yeah." The word came out breathy and meek. What an impressive dominant grizzly shifter she made.

Damon blinked slowly, then shook his head and dragged his attention back to the papers in his hand. "I can see you aren't up for the contract, so I'll bid you ado."

Her legs felt like bouncy springs as she stumbled toward the chair and plopped down into it. "Obviously my answer is 'no' to bearing your…offspring. Gross word. But I'm curious about your pitch. Am I the first woman you've proposed this to?"

"Males of my species traditionally raise the offspring—"

"Why is that?"

A blaze of emotion struck through Damon's eyes like a flash of lightning, there and gone before his face was a mask of passive indifference again. "Because the females all die during childbirth."

"Oh. Well, that sounds hellish. What kind of shifter are you?"

Another soft, growling rumble vibrated against her skin, so she clamped her mouth shut and reached her hand out.

His eyes narrowed, but he stood and leaned over his desk, then set the paperwork gently into her palm. Across the top, it read *Binding Contract*.

"Do you usually let Mason choose your conquests?"

Damon was quiet for a long time as he studied her face before he said, "No. He's never brought me a female before. I usually choose who to interview."

"Why did he start with me?"

Damon shook his head slowly, apparently unwilling to answer.

"Fine, who's Feyadine?"

"Ms. Sutterfield, I think it's best if you go now." The use of her formal name hurt in ways she couldn't explain. "I'll pay you double whatever Mason offered you for your trouble, but this won't work."

She huffed a laugh and nodded, then stood. "Just as well. I've already tried the doctors, and they couldn't do anything for me."

"You want a child?" he asked abruptly.

"Don't worry about paying me double," she said, biting back stinging tears as she strode for the door. "I don't want your money."

"Ms. Sutterfield. Clara!"

She turned, lip trembling as she allowed him to see the anger in her eyes.

"What is the tattoo on your shoulder?"

"A dragon." Tortured, she swallowed hard and then admitted in a whisper, "I dream of them." Then she turned and pulled on the door handle, and this time, it opened easily. She shut the door behind her and jogged down the echoing hallway toward Mason, who waited by the suit of armor. His expression was bleak and sad.

Shattering glass echoed from the office, and the house rattled with a deafening roar. The noise filled her head, so Clara covered her ears to save her sensitive eardrums as she ran.

That sound held such pain. More pain than any man ought to hold.

Damon Daye said ghosts didn't bother men

like him.
    Damon Daye had lied.

THREE

Damon gripped his stomach and willed his dragon to stay inside of him. His office was no place to Change. And yet the rage that unfurled within him, the loss, devastation, hope, longing, and crippling loneliness were too much to bear. Was this what it was like to die?

He'd imagined it so many times over the eons. Passing from this world to the next, meeting his family and friends in the beyond was a dream he would never realize. Not him, the last immortal dragon. And yet there she'd stood, his Feyadine in the form of a quirky young woman with an exact tattoo of her people's crest. Down to her blood and bone, Clara was a Blackwing. She was ancestor to his enemies and the exact physical replica of his beloved Feyadine, seer to the last of the Blackwings.

"Fuck," he gritted out as he glared at the priceless vase he'd shattered against the wall. Emotion was a poison to dragons like him. Mortal dragons could afford to feel. They only had one life to suffer through, but him? Feeling cut like blades against his insides for eternity.

Breathing heavy, he stared at the door. She wanted a baby, had visited doctors for a baby. Mason would've kept her profile with the other potential breeding females. Damon stood and ran for the filing cabinets in a hidden panel of the wall. He slammed his palm against the lever and waited impatiently for the barrier to slide open. His heart hammered double-time against his sternum as he rifled through the potential breeders. *There.* He yanked Clara Sutterfield's file from a section marked *Feyadine's line. Never contact.*

It was right there in her lineage. A long genealogy dating back to a hybrid shifter fathered by Feyadine's brother, Nall. There was a reason he'd made the rule never to search for Feyadine's ancestors. One that kept his heart safe from what was happening to him now. He'd spiraled for centuries after he'd lost her, and now it was happening all over again. He rested his back against the wall as he read Clara's file.

Clara wasn't just a risk to him.

She was a risk to the whole damned world. The last time he'd suffered the loss of a Blackwing mate, Damon had annihilated the remainder of his species and blackened the earth with dragon's fire.

"I'll find you again," Feyadine had promised.

Perhaps she had.

****

"You let me walk in there thinking I was going to evict ghosts!" she yelled at Mason. "How could you do that? How could you let me go into that mess unprepared?"

"I'm so sorry. I just didn't know what else to tell you to get you here."

"What is he, Mason?"

"I can't tell you."

Clara slammed her palms against the Towncar and shook her head, so angry she could spit nails. Preferably at Mason's head.

She wanted to rage and cry all at once, and for what? She didn't know Damon.

"Take me back to the airport."

"Clara, if you'll just give him time—"

"To what? Put a monster baby in me?"

"But you want a child anyway!"

"How do you know? How do you know

anything about me?"

"Because I've been tracking you for years. I know about your crew. I know about the doctors. I know everything! Now is the time, and I was right, wasn't I? You felt something when you laid eyes on him for the first time. I saw it on your face. There was something there, hanging in the air between you."

"Why the fuck does it matter to you?"

"Because he has a chance to be good!" Mason chucked his driver's hat, and it sailed across the perfectly manicured front lawn. "Godammit, woman. He has a chance to be good. You're his chance. He's ready. And don't ask me how I know. I just do."

"Take me away from here," she gritted out, voice quavering. She yanked open the back door and crawled in, then waited for him to finally unhook his hands from his hips and get behind the wheel.

"You're making a mistake," he murmured, holding her gaze in the rearview mirror.

"You don't know me, Mason, and it's become abundantly clear that no matter what you think, you don't really know that man in there either. I'm nobody's chance to be good."

Clara forced herself not to look out the back window as Mason drove her away. She'd learned long ago that looking back was weakness. To survive, she needed to look ahead. Always. Regret, revisiting the past, pondering what-ifs was a waste of time reserved for people who had lost a lot less than her.

When a flash of the smiling hazel-eyed child from the plane rippled across her mind, she slammed her head back against the seat and closed her eyes. What a cruel twist of fate that she would have a child dangled in front of her, yet again. She pulled her floral duffle to her stomach and clutched it like the comfort blanket she'd had as a kid. Mason kept looking at her in the rearview with an unfathomable expression. Let him. What did she care? Clara looked out the window as the pristine cobblestone driveway morphed into a dirt road beneath the tires.

"This isn't the way we came up here," she growled out.

"It's shorter this way, and besides, I think it would be good for you to see Damon isn't a monster. He's done a lot of good for these mountains and the people in them."

She sighed a put-upon sound and narrowed her eyes at a break in the trees. Through the opening, she could see miles of rolling pine forest. None of this would change her mind, but she was exhausted from whatever had happened between her and Damon, the headache was still lingering, and frankly, she didn't care how Mason got her out of these mountains and back to the airport, so long as he did. And she definitely wasn't up for another row with the pig-headed man quietly driving her down a switchback.

The scenery really was breathtaking. Clara leaned against the glass and pressed both hands on the window, just to leave smudges and feel as though she'd won a tiny battle. Outside, evergreens, ferns, wild grasses, brambles, and wildflowers painted a wilderness canvas full of colors too vibrant to be real. It was springtime, and apparently the rains that had been coasting across the country had done this place good.

Mason drove her past a flat cliff ledge where curious, giant machines stood still and abandoned, the arm of one stuck in the air as if its operator had stopped mid-chore when they cut out for the workday.

"Damon owns these mountains," Mason said.

"Of course he does."

A muscle twitched in Mason's jaw. Good.

She hoped she was as annoying to him as he was to her.

"Several years ago, pine beetles started killing off the trees. Mostly the weak and old ones at first, but that's what happened to all the dead ones you see."

Outside, there was a mash-up of brown interspersed in the green. Dead trees, and all because of a bug. Huh.

"Mr. Daye has a protective nature, so he began gathering in these mountains shifters he respected to cut down the dead lumber and replant as they went along. There are three crews that live here. The Ashe Crew, the Gray Backs, and the Boarlanders. They clear the land in sections and deliver the lumber to the Lowlander Crew, who own the sawmill down in Saratoga. Gorilla shifters, and real hard workers. It helps Damon keep his land healthy, and in turn, he gives these folks who don't fit anywhere else jobs and homes."

It was then that she saw the sign over the road. *Grayland Mobile Park*. Mason slowed and came to a stop in front of a high, bricked fire pit where several people were gathered around a grill, talking and laughing. Behind them was a semi-circle of singlewide trailers. Clara couldn't guess their age since they'd been covered in cedar shingles and fixed up with screened-in porches. All but the one on the end. That one had a new porch built off the side, but the trailer itself looked less cared for than the others. Chipped cream paint and green shudders, a splintered front door that looked as if some sort of rodent had tried to chew its way through, and the numbers beside the doorframe were barely hanging on by a rusty, bent-up nail. *1010*. Chills blasted up her arms, and she rubbed them to bring warmth back into her skin.

"Why are we stopping?" she asked as a tall man without a shirt approached. His entire torso was covered with crisscrossing scars, but he wore a greeting smile.

Ignoring her, Mason rolled down his window and gave the guy a mannish handshake. One of those that ended with a fist bump. Hmm. Maybe Mason wasn't as big a fuddy-duddy as she'd deemed him. "Hey, Matt," Mason greeted through an answering grin.

Matt leaned onto the door frame, big triceps flexing as he asked, "You here to party with the riff-raff? Get on out here. We have brisket cooking and beer on ice." The blue-eyed man's nostrils flared, and he slid a gaze to the back seat. "Holy shit, you've got a crier."

Mortified by his observation, Clara wiped her eyes.

"Willa!" he called behind him. "I can't do tears, Nerd. This one is all you. Mason, get your ass out of the car and grab a drink."

Mason tossed her a cocky grin, rolled up the window and kicked his door open as Matt sauntered back to the others.

"Where are you going?"

"To party with the riff-raff." Mason pocketed the keys and shut the driver-side door. "You can come out here and meet the Gray Backs and eat some delicious barbecue, or you can stay in there and pout."

"Sea cucumber shifters are assholes," she called as he walked away.

"Boar shifter," he called over his shoulder.

Clara crossed her arms over her chest and growled. Sea cucumber, boar, or hamster, the man was still a grade-A douche-wagon.

She startled when a tiny woman with black, thick-rimmed glasses and hair dyed an unnatural shade of bright red opened the door right next to her. She sniffed the air and grinned, then pointed her finger at Clara. "Werebear."

Clara huffed a surprised laugh and scented

the air. The mini-woman was also a bear shifter, and a dominant female, like herself. Respect. "Werebear," she drawled.

"I'm Willa, and I'm coming in because I've never been in Damon's car and those jackasses are going to be so jealous."

"I'm Clara."

Willa climbed over her lap and shut the door, then wiggled to the front and hit the lock button right as a dark-haired man lifted the door handle. "Hey! I want to see in there, too."

"Back off, Jason. I'll paint you a picture later."

Jason jiggled the handle with a miffed expression that marred his handsome features. "Now that's just *rude*," he huffed as he released the door and stomped off.

Clara was trying not to laugh, because really, she wanted to hold onto her anger for a little while longer, but Willa opened the cap of a tiny liquor bottle from a hidden mini bar and handed it to her. "One for you and one for me and— *I will eat you!*" she yelled when Jason tried the door one last time.

When he cupped his hands over his eyebrows and stared into the dark tinted window, Clara told him blandly, "I'm crying."

"Ew, no." Jason left and didn't look back.

"Nicely done. Girl tears. Sends men skittering away every time. Cheers," Willa said through a bright grin as she held up her miniature bottle of vodka.

Clara tinked hers against Willa's and shook her head before she slammed the shot of throat-scorching liquid. Why the hell not? She could use a stiff drink after the day she'd had.

"Sooo, Clara Beara, why ya cryin'?" Willa asked, slouching back in the seat and resting her rainbow converse sneakers on the headrest in front of her.

Clara pursed her lips, uninterested in sharing how naïve she'd been. "Why are you wearing glasses? Bears shifters have excellent vision."

"Oh, these." Willa shoved them farther up her nose, nerd-style. "Matt, my mate, is into real geeky shit, so when I want him frisky, I pull out the glasses. They have no magnification. They're for sex-appeal only."

"Huh. I like that," Clara admitted as the edges of her vision went fuzzy, and she got that weightless feeling only a good shot of vodka could give her.

"What's this?" Willa asked, pulling the rumpled binding contract from Clara's lap.

That damning paperwork should've been

embarrassing, but she would never see Willa again after today, and frankly, Mason had turned off her give-a-damn switch. "That would be part of the reason I'm crying."

"Big dominant grizzly shifter brought to tears by paper," Willa murmured, flipping to the second page with a distracted look as she read. "Holy shit. Is this what I think it is? And ew, please tell me his pitch didn't actually involve him calling you a breeder."

"That's me. Breeder to…whatever terrifying shifter Damon is."

Willa's eyebrows arched high, and her chestnut brown eyes went round. "Dragon, boo. This is a contract to boink the last immortal dragon."

Clara gripped the empty bottle in her hand as if the tiny thing would anchor her to this world. "I'm sorry. I just thought you said dragon."

"Like that sexpot tattoo you're rockin' on your shoulder blade. Fire fire, pew pew."

"He breathes fire?"

"Uh, Clara," Willa said in a business tone as she smoothed the contract over her lap. "Why, perchance, has Mason brought you here?"

"Probably to try and convince me to stay. And because he's a dick bent on ruining this day even further."

Willa cleared her throat and pointed to a tall man with jet black hair and dark eyes. He looked vaguely familiar, but Clara couldn't put her finger on why until Willa explained, "That's my alpha, Creed, and he's related to Damon. I'd bet my worms Mason brought you here to get any questions you have answered by that man."

Clara narrowed her eyes at the driver, who had shimmied out of his suit jacket and rolled his sleeves up to his forearms. He was currently tilting his head back and glugging a beer as though he hadn't just tricked her into traveling all the way from Florida to be a rental womb for a freaking *dragon*. She was the queen of being dooped. "Son of a biscuit eater."

"Mmm, I love biscuits," Willa murmured, but when Clara looked over at her, Willa was staring at Matt with a hungry smile.

On that note, Clara unlocked the door and slipped out of the car, determined not to let Mason win whatever game he was playing.

A beer and some brisket, and she would be on her way back to Florida and well on her way to putting this mortifying situation behind her.

FOUR

Clara liked the Gray Backs. No, like was too soft a word. She freaking adored them. They were funny and gave each other so much shit, but underneath all the bravado, here was a crew of people who really cared about each other. A crew who had chosen each other to walk through this crazy life together. They reminded her of her own crew—a dangerous thought, so she popped a last bite of baked beans into her maw and tossed her plate in a trash bag attached to the side of the buffet table near the grill. The evening sun had disappeared, dousing them in darkness. Jason had turned on strands of outdoor lights that had been draped all over the trailer park, and the fire gave enough of a glow that she could see every face around it clearly. Already, they'd been shooting the shit for an hour. Clara didn't have to talk much, but she was enjoying figuring out the dynamics.

Willa called herself the "almost alpha," while Creed, the actual alpha, was the strong, patient type. His mate Gia was tall and curvy and was always rocking their baby girl, even though the infant was asleep already. She must be used to the rowdy crew to sleep through such noise. Matt hovered around Willa like a planet to a sun, and Jason and his park ranger mate didn't go two minutes without touching each other. Clara was pretty sure they didn't even notice they were doing it. They just reached out and brushed each other's hands or shoulders just to reassure their animals their mate was fine. Aviana was a shy, dark-headed woman who twitched her head strangely when she was amused. A bird shifter of some sort, Clara would guess, because she definitely didn't smell like a bear. And then there was Aviana's mate, Beaston. Oh, she liked the strange man with a deep limp to his stride. He had wild, bright green eyes and looked terrifying in the firelight, but made it clear with every strange combination of words he uttered how deeply he felt everything and how infinitely he cared about his people. He was an enigma she wanted to figure out. A puzzle with missing pieces that had been forced together to create something even more interesting.

"Let's prank call Damon," Willa said, poking buttons on her cell phone.

Clara's eyes flew wide, and she shook her head. "I think that's a bad idea."

"Agreed, it's a great idea." Willa lifted the phone to her ear. Shhh, she mouthed, flapping her hand to quiet everyone down. "What do they say about atoms?" She waited with a vacant grin on her face. "Never trust 'em. They make up everything!"

"Dork jokes?" Matt scoffed, snatching the phone. "Let a pro handle this. Hey, Damon, is your refrigerator running?" Matt grinned at Clara across the fire. "Well, you better go catch it!"

The Gray Backs and Mason all groaned in unison. Willa jerked the phone away from her mate and back to her ear. "Hey, Damon, you're Womb for Hire is down in the Grayland Mobile Park getting sloshed. Better come get her before she makes horrible life decisions." Willa hung up the phone, and the firelight reflected off her grin.

"I've had one beer," Clara argued as her cheeks flushed with heat. "And a little bit of vodka, but I'm not making any horrible life decisions tonight or any other night." He wouldn't come down from his house for her. It was late at night, and Damon didn't give two craps about her. Womb for Hire was right. She was nothing more to the man.

Clara looked over at baby Rowan, still asleep in her mother's arms beside her, but couldn't bear it for long so she ripped her gaze away and picked at the edge of the label on her beer.

"Do you want to hold her?" Gia asked.

"Really?" Clara asked, trying to stifle the hope in her voice.

"Yeah." Gia stood from her neon green plastic chair and settled Rowan in Clara's arms.

"Ooooh," Clara said on a breath as she moved the corner of the baby blanket away from Rowan's face. "She's precious."

"You know," Creed said thoughtfully, "if you're wanting a baby, you could do much worse than Damon as your child's father. You and your baby would never want for anything."

"And he would be the safest kid on the planet," Matt chimed in. "Bullies at school? Daddy Damon would swoop down and eat—"

Willa nudged him hard.

"Eat what?" Clara asked, searching their faces one by one. They'd all gone comically blank, even Mason's. "Eat what?" she repeated, louder.

Beaston met her eye. "Damon protects the Gray Backs and the Boarlanders. Damon protects the Ashe Crew. Even C-team, he gobbles up our enemies." Beaston relaxed into his chair, slipping his arm easily over Aviana's shoulders beside him. With a predatory smile, he murmured, "Chomp."

Clara sighed, utterly disturbed. "Fantastic. And if I could get over all the fire-breathing, people-eating, romancelessness of all of this, I can't even imagine what having an actual dragon baby would be like. Or egg? Do dragons hatch from eggs?"

Gia giggled and shook her head. "Your child would be a hybrid and mortal, so no hatching from an egg. If you want to imagine what a dragon shifter child looks like, look down. You're holding one."

Clara's face went slack in surprise, and she jerked her gaze down to tiny Rowan in her arms.

"Someday," Beaston said, "our Rowan is going to be a fierce Gray Back. Silver scales and fire. Good to her bones because her parents are good to their bones. You would be lucky to mother a dragon."

"But honestly," Creed said, his dark eyebrows arched high, "you'll probably have a bear cub. Baby dragons are rare. Damon probably has your odds written out in your paperwork."

Mason shook his head and warned Creed with his eyes.

"My paperwork?"

"The...file he has on...you?"

"Shut. Up," Mason muttered out the side of his mouth.

"No matter," Clara gritted out, choking the neck of her beer bottle. She would not let this ruin the otherwise enjoyable night. Nor would she imagine what kind of dirt they'd dug up for that file because she would not be here to—

Whoosh!

Something enormous flew overhead, pushing the air down until the trees around the trailer park bent and cracked. The fire blew out, and Clara huddled her body over Rowan's to protect her as the others scrambled around her. For an instant, it felt like a hurricane, and then the pressure was gone. Rowan fussed in her arms, so Clara handed the baby back to Gia.

"What the hell was that?" she asked, searching the woods for danger as her instincts kicked up to survival mode. The fine hairs on her body were electrified.

"That would be your beau coming to protect you from those horrible life decisions," Willa said.

Matt and Jason rushed to re-light the fire while Creed righted a pair of toppled lawn chairs. And by the time the glow of the firelight was illuminating the trailer park once again, Damon himself stepped from the woods wearing dark dress pants. He was still fastening up the top few buttons of his white oxford shirt.

"Wait, did you bring a change of clothes for your Shift?" Jason asked. "Like, you carried a suit in your gigantic claws and flew through the air with it?"

"Don't make it weird." Damon lifted his churning, silver gaze to Clara. She could've sworn she saw worry in his features, but it couldn't be because he still wore his mask of indifference. But... he did look different somehow.

"Are you all right?" he asked in a clear,

steady timbre as he approached her.

"Oh, my God," Willa said, clasping her hands in front of her face and smiling all mushy. "It's like one of my romance books. *The Zillionaire Dragon's Baby*."

"Willa," Damon warned low.

"*Ravished by Her Dragon*," Gia murmured helpfully.

Willa laughed and said, "*Clara Beara and her Scaly Boinker*."

Damon sighed a long, irritated sound, which only seemed to push Willa on.

"*The Dragon's Honey Pot. Daddy Dragon Wants a Zygote*."

"Willa," Damon repeated, his eyes tightening in the firelight.

Softly, she whispered, "*Bear Boobs and Dragon Diddles*."

"I would read the shit out of that," Beaston said.

"You would!" Willa rounded on him. "And by the way, I know it's you whose been stealing all my romance books."

Beaston shrugged unapologetically and corrected, "Borrow, not steal."

Aviana's shoulders were shaking with laughter behind him. And when Clara giggled too loud, she covered it with a delicate cough.

If she didn't know for a fact the last immortal dragon was grumpy and didn't smile, she would've sworn he'd just cracked one. And in that flash of an instant, it had been mesmerizing. Straight white teeth behind those sensual lips, and dimples that she wanted to curl up and fall asleep in and oh, her ovaries were doing a fireworks show with trumpets playing in the background. And now he was looking at her like she was a weirdo with her mouth hanging open—probably because she *was* a weirdo with her mouth hanging open. He leaned over a smiling Gia, kissing her on the cheek in a sweet greeting as he took baby Rowan from her arms, and damn it all, Clara's ovaries were nothing but mushroom clouds now.

Damon freaking Daye was as hot as the fire he breathed.

He held Rowan against his chest and cooed, "Brave little dragon. Did I wake you?" He bounced slightly and rocked from side to side, and within moments, Rowan had given up her fussing and was clinging to Damon's pointer finger with one chubby fist and looking up at him with round eyes as dark as Creed's. Fair skin and dark eyes to match the black crop of hair on her tiny dome.

A mellow rumble sounded from within Damon, but it wasn't the scary growls he'd emitted earlier. This was a satisfied sound. One of contentment as he studied the baby's face and rocked her. The Gray Backs had gone quiet as they watched Damon lose himself in the little girl's gaze. Slowly, he leaned down and smelled Rowan's breath, then smiled and murmured, "Tiny fire breather." And then there it was again—that heart-stopping smile. Here and gone, but she'd seen it.

Damon handed Rowan back to Gia, but by the time his silver gaze landed on Clara, his features had turned to stone again. "Can I speak with you? Alone?"

And just like that, all her mushy feelings evaporated at the coldness of his tone. "Fine." She turned and sauntered off toward the tree line. Just inside the woods, where she could still see the light from the trailer park, Clara turned and waited.

Here it came. Bossy Damon was going to scold her for Willa prank-calling him and then chastise her for drinking too much. *Lay it on me, grumpy dragon.*

"I'm sorry," he said in a low, gravelly voice.

Clara opened her mouth to give him a seething retort, but stopped herself just in time. "Wait, what?"

"I'm sorry for being so harsh with you earlier."

"You aren't mad about the prank call?"

Damon huffed a laugh and almost smiled again. "No, I didn't mind. I was awake anyway, though I was surprised to hear you were still here. I thought you were long gone."

"Mason is full of tricks."

He arched on eyebrow pointedly and looked over his shoulder at his driver sitting by the fire. "He had tricks for us both."

"Sooo, you aren't mad that you had to fly down here on account of me drinking too much?"

"Why would I be? You're a grown woman. It's good to cut loose every once in a while and besides, I like…"

She dipped her voice to a whisper. "You like what?"

Damon frowned and cleared his throat. "It's late, and it's a long drive to the airport from here." He placed his hands behind his back and straightened his spine. "I'd like to extend an invitation for you to stay the night in one of my guest rooms. If you still wish it, you can leave in the morning." *Or not.* That last part he didn't have to say. The unspoken words hung in the air between them.

"That would be nice."

"Yes?" His eyebrows jacked up in surprise.

"Well, it is late, and I've had about all I can take of Mason for the day. I'll leave in the morning."

Damon cut his gaze to the others, then nodded his head once. The silver in his eyes was fading by the second, leaving them as dark as the night sky. He turned to leave, but Clara grabbed his hand, not wanting to end this moment with him. The second her fingertips touched his palm, a blinding pain blasted through her head and drew a gasp from her lips. Squeezing her eyes tightly closed, Clara pressed her hands to her temples as if that would keep her head from splitting apart.

I'll love you always.

You won't. You can't. You love me now only because you haven't seen the monster I am yet.

Clara.

"Clara!" Damon gripped her shoulders and bent his knees until he was eye-level with her. "Are you all right?"

Clara drew a deep, shaking breath and shook off the remnants of the headache. That was weird. Usually her headaches lasted longer, but that one had been a flash of pain, and now…nothing.

She gripped his wrists and searched his dark eyes. "You're warm. I expected you to be cold as stone."

His grip on her shoulders lessened and he let off a tiny, relieved breath. "I run too warm. It hurts…"

"You?" she guessed. She wished he would finish his thoughts so she could understand him.

"No. I hurt other people." His eyes tightened, and he looked away as though he was about to leave, so she wrapped her arms around his waist before she could change her mind. Damon stood frozen under her hug. Not a muscle twitched, not a joint moved. His hands hovered out to his sides, but she didn't care. Clara pressed her cheek against his chest. Yes, he was warm. Warmer than bears. Her cheek heated on that side, like a blush, but to the point she would have to pull away soon. That felt tragic, separating.

Wait, what was she doing? She wasn't supposed to be doing this. Hugging Damon wasn't going to help her leave any easier. But his body relaxed under her, and his hands slid up her back. One stayed pressed against her spine, while the other traveled up and up until

Damon gripped the back of her neck. So warm. So safe. A shiver traveled up her back and landed in her shoulders. Here headache was back. Not painful, but pulsing in the middle of her head, reminding her that she could be incapacitated at any moment.

"I'm sorry," she whispered, forcing herself to ease away. "I don't know why I did that. I'm not usually a hugger."

"Nor am I." Damon's head was cocked, and he stared at her as if he was a scientist studying something he couldn't understand. "Would you like to stay here for a while, or do you want to go back to my house?"

"You would stay here if I wanted to?"

Damon dipped his chin once.

"Mason said the Gray Backs work for you."

"A shifter like me can't afford to have friends, Ms. Sutterfield, but if I did, the Gray Backs would be some of them. I don't mind spending more time here if that is what you desire."

"Desire, huh? So do dragons give wishes like genies?"

A slow smile spread across his face, and his eyes sparked. "What kind of wish do you need granted?"

"I *desire* for you to shotgun a beer with

me."

Both of his dark eyebrows jacked up this time. "Shotgun a beer?"

"Yeah, you know. Poke a hole in the bottom of a beer can, pop the top, and chug it like the super un-boring dragon you are. I can rub you like a genie if you want," she teased, waggling her eyebrows.

Damon's eyes narrowed in the soft glow of the firelight. "Minx."

"Wish granted?"

"Creed," Damon called at normal volume over his shoulder. "Do you have cans of beer, and can you teach me the art of shotgunning?"

The Gray Backs went dead quiet for an instant before their chatter picked up at double volume.

"Hell yes," Creed crowed.

Damon stepped out of her path and gestured toward the fire, palm up as he bowed. "After you."

Okay, so Clara hadn't really thought he would say yes. She was teasing, thinking an immortal would've lost their sense of adventure along the eons, but Damon was apparently up for playing. He'd shocked her to her bones, and damn, it had been a long time since someone had surprised her.

The Gray Backs, as it turned out, were all down to shotgun beers, and so they gathered around the fire pit, Bud Lights in hand, as Creed explained the technical side to poking a hole in the bottom. This was Willa, Georgia, and Aviana's first shotgun, too, so Damon was in good company. Clara watched him relax and laugh with the Gray Backs as he prepared his beer, and in that moment, everything faded away. The background became blurry and dull while Damon drew up into focus. His muscular shoulders pressed against the crisp white material of his shirt, and his Adam's apple bobbed as he swallowed and prepared to pop the top of his beverage.

"One!" Willa said with the happiest grin on her face.

From the way the Gray Backs acted, Damon didn't cut loose with them often.

"Two!"

Clara jammed her finger under the top of her can. Her breath halted as Damon turned that demon-black gaze on her and mouthed, *Are you ready?* Heart-stopping smile. Heart. Stopping.

"Three!"

With a giggle, she popped the top of her drink and chugged her beer from the hole near the bottom. She spilled everywhere, but most of it got into her. She leaned over, cracking up as she wiped her mouth. Damon didn't spill a drop. Of course, he was good at shotgunning. She'd bet he was good at everything he tried.

He took her empty can like a true gentleman and disposed of it, then returned with a proud smile. He nodded his head magnanimously and drew her hand to his lips, then murmured, "Wish granted." Lifting a hungry gaze to hers, he whispered, "And you didn't even have to rub me."

Clara's breath froze in her throat. The naughty man wasn't as cold as she'd supposed. He knew how to tease her back. And as he dropped her hand and turned to say something low to Creed, who was clapping him on the back, Clara blinked slowly and had to focus on staying upright. Her legs had turned to noodles when he had brushed his lips across her knuckles. It was an old fashioned kiss, yes, but a kiss just the same, and now her stomach dipped as if she were falling.

But for the life of her, she couldn't figure out if it was good to fall for a man like Damon Daye, or epically bad.

FIVE

A smile lingered on Damon's lips as he looked out the window of the Towncar. It was dark outside, but his night vision was impeccable. Every branch and every pine needle, every set of reflective animal eyes and every blade of wild grass was as crisp and clear as it would be in the daytime.

Turning his head slightly, he snuck a glance at Clara, but she was watching him, too. Busted. Her answering smile turned shy, and she dropped her gaze to the hem of her shirt, which she was fiddling with.

Mason suddenly had nothing to say and, sure as anything, Damon was going to deal with him tomorrow, but right now, he had this tiny tangle of giddiness in his gut. Shotgunning a beer. Truly? Damon shook his head and tried to get a grip on the stupid smile tugging at his lips. What was the woman doing to him? Daring him to step out of his comfort zone with that beautiful challenge in her dancing green eyes, and like a lovesick adolescent, he'd risen to the dare just to see that smile on her full lips. Hers was a smile he would fell entire mountains for.

She was nothing like Feyadine.

Feyadine had been shy and had trouble speaking her mind, while this wild creature could look him directly in the eyes and tell him exactly what she was thinking. And her hair. Red like his flames and curled into little corkscrews. Feyadine's had been a darker auburn, and she'd kept hers pulled tightly back in pins, as was the style at the time. Her eyes were also gray instead of the clear mossy green of Clara's. And if those differences weren't enough, the second Clara opened her mouth, there was no mistaking her with Feyadine.

And yet Damon had that same kind of pulse-pounding, dick-hardening response he'd had to Feyadine all those centuries ago. This was all confusing, and though he'd never admit it aloud, terrifying.

It would be best for everyone when she left in the morning.

The thought of losing her before he got to know more about her made his dragon unfurl uncomfortably in his middle. A single click cracked inside his chest. A warning from his firestarter that he needed to settle down or this car would go up in flames, and its inhabitants along with it. And as much as Damon wanted to pretend Mason and Clara meant nothing to him, he'd been trying to change since his mistakes with Diem. When he'd hurt his daughter, his son-in-law, Bruiser, had given him a verbal beat-down that opened his eyes to so much. And from that day forward, he'd begun to *feel* for the people who worked in his mountains.

Feeling and caring were agony for a shifter like him because like all the rest, his friends would age, wither, and die. And he would bury them one by one and break all over again. Weak. He was weak to let mortals affect him, and yet he couldn't tame his attachment to them. Not anymore.

"Can I tell you something and you forget it in the morning?" Clara asked so low he almost missed it.

He nodded once, curiosity piqued.

"I like your smile. You seem like a man who doesn't give it often, and I felt special tonight that you gave it to me."

Damon inhaled deeply. Fuck.

"I'm not a good man to get attached to, Ms. Sutterfield." God he hated uttering her surname. He had to distance himself, but really he wanted to put his mouth around her real name. Clara. Beautiful, wild, strong Clara. Dangerous Clara.

Her face fell, and she looked out her window, hiding those vivid eyes from him. Pain slashed through his middle. He would have to hurt her a lot more if she didn't stop knocking on the stony walls of his heart. The game she played could kill everything he'd built.

"Do you know what the tattoo on your shoulder blade symbolizes?" Of course, she did. It was the perfect replica of the Blackwing's crest, down to the most minute detail and line work. She'd researched her lineage.

"No. It's just a picture I get in my head." She was still hiding her gaze, staring at the passing evergreens as they bumped and bounced up the dirt road toward his home.

Damon frowned. "Where have you seen it before?" Perhaps there were scrolls from her genealogy that she'd found.

She swung her gaze to him, and he could see it now. Honesty pooling deep in her eyes. "I told you I see it in my head. I get these headaches, and then I get these flashes of...something." Her voice dipped to a wisp of breath. "Teeth and fire and wings."

A seer then. A true seer, not the untalented psychic she fancied herself. Clara was housing great power to draw on images that far past.

"What do you see?"

"I-I can't say."

"Can't or won't?" Why wouldn't she tell him? What was she hiding?

"Can't. I don't understand the images. They're just these insane pictures that make no sense. Like a mash-up. A collage of unrelated instances that don't tell any story. I'm going mad." Clara gasped. "I didn't mean to say that last part."

"Explain it now."

"Do you always get what you want? A simple please would get you a long way."

"Yes."

"Yes what?"

"Yes, I always get what I want. And please, explain it now."

When Clara narrowed her eyes to dangerous-looking slits, chills blasted up his arms. Little mortal hellion. She would've made an intimidating adversary in the dragon wars.

"My grandma went crazy with what she called the sight. Dreams and headaches and visions of awful things. She was stark raving mad by the time she passed. Clawing at the walls of a padded room and screaming about monsters that had eaten each other up. I'm the same as her. I'll have the same fate. I already feel myself slipping into these visions. They feel so real I think I have some kind of connection to a different dimension or something. That's how it starts, you know? Thinking your hallucinations are real. I even bought into my own hype so much that I sank all of my savings into a crappy store in a shopping center where I read palms and tarot cards. I even have a crystal ball. Pretty lame, huh?"

"Mmm," he said noncommittally. If she didn't know her own power, he wasn't going to enlighten her on how dangerous she could be.

His response had been wrong because Clara's shoulders slumped, and she leaned against the door, far away from him. Before he could change his mind, he asked, "Why did you hug me?"

"Because it felt right." Her answer was quick and honest.

"Why?"

"Because you feel safe. Stupid, right? More proof I'm broken and so are my instincts. You're a dragon, and yet I haven't felt so comfortable since…"

"Since what? Finish it. Please."

"Since my crew." When she looked at him, her eyes were filled with such sadness, he had to look away. He'd read her file and knew the bare bones of what she'd been through. She'd been an alpha once.

Damon wanted to hold her hand. He wanted to touch her. Kiss her until she forgot all about the sadness. He knew about losing someone. He knew all about insides being ripped up. He couldn't do anything to save the people he had loved over the centuries. With just a despairing look at him, she'd reminded him how heavy the burden of loneliness could be. Dangerous Clara. Clenching his hands against the urge to pull her against his side, he did the only thing he knew how. He pushed her away. "You're right, Ms. Sutterfield. Your instincts are broken."

****

Clara sat there stunned. The smile had

faded from Damon's face, and his eyes glinted dangerously in the dark. His expression had morphed into the stoic mask where she couldn't tell if he liked or loathed her. It was the face he wore the most, and she hated it.

When Mason pulled the car to a stop in front of Damon's house, the dragon dropped his gaze and shoved out of the car. "Mason," he barked out, "see her to her room." And then he disappeared inside.

Numbly, Clara followed the now quiet driver through the front doors. She followed him down the cold marble hallway that seemed to stretch for miles. She followed him past statues and fountains, past winding staircases and what looked like an old-fashioned ballroom. Sconces and chandeliers and wooden doors stretched to three times her height, and it all combined to give her a single feeling—frigid emptiness. Damon had decorated this place without any warmth at all.

Perhaps it was he who was broken.

Mason adjusted the strap of her duffle bag on his shoulder and shoved open a heavy wooden door that had been painted a cream color. The paint was worn and chipped, and it looked as if it had been taken from some ancient castle. Inside, the guestroom was bigger than her entire apartment in Florida. There was white wainscoting along the walls, and intricate crown molding around every window and along the entirety of the ceiling. Above the wainscoting was wallpaper in a mauve floral print that should've felt outdated and dull, but paired with the four poster bed with the gauze curtains, the room looked quite elegant and comfortable. There was a sitting area, and a set of French doors were open to a sprawling balcony that overlooked the waterfall she'd seen earlier.

It was a room fit for a queen, and Clara was definitely trailing trailer-park dirt all over the pristine dark wood floors.

Surprised by the contrast to the sterile white corridors, she murmured, "This room is so different than the rest of the house."

Mason nodded and smiled, then pointed to a room off the main and said, "The bathroom is through there. Sleep as late as you like." He hovered at the doorway where he'd set her bag down as if he wanted to say more, but turned abruptly instead and closed the door behind him, leaving her alone in the enormous room.

The shower was roughly the size of her

bedroom at home, and when she finally figured out how to turn on the hot tap, water fell like rain from the ceiling. She washed the travel dirt from her skin and towel dried her hair, then readied for bed in a daze. Her mind circled around Damon, from the contract to him breaking the glass in his office, from his agonized roar to the Grayland Mobile Park, and then back—always back—to that stunning dimple-smile he'd given over and over again tonight. He was the most interesting, yet confounding man she'd ever met. And even more terrifying than her interest in a cold man was the bone-deep desire that unfurled in her belly anytime he was around. She was giving him the power to hurt her, and for what? She hadn't known him long enough to care about what made him tick.

Clara closed the terrace doors, turned off the lights, and buried herself under the plush covers of the bed. With a frown, she looked over at the wall beside her. What if he was there on the other side? She didn't know for sure, but she could almost sense him, almost picture him, restless in his own bed, as she was in hers.

She scooted to the side of the bed she imagined was closest to him and relaxed. It was there that she drifted off, as close to the cold dragon as she would ever sleep.

Pain, sharp and bright.
Clara squeezed her eyes closed, then opened them again as the ache in her head subsided. Where was she? She looked down at her hands, clasped tightly in her lap. Her crossed legs were covered with green silk that shone in the candlelight. She wore a dress, but none like she'd ever seen. It was full in the skirts and tight from her waist up. Her sleeves were nothing more than lace caps right at the tips of her collar bones. Her headache was probably because her hair was pulled too tight in the pins that were jabbing into her head. Baffled, she looked around. The room was dark, and the walls made of stone. It was dark, like a cave, and old-fashioned lanterns hung from the walls on rusty pegs. Above was a large, circular chandelier, but instead of lightbulbs, it housed hundreds of lit candles, dripping wax onto the large table beneath. And around that table stood tall, broad-shouldered men, talking low. They spoke in a language she shouldn't understand, but did, and all of the men, warriors if their dress and manners were anything to go by, deferred to one man who

stood closest to her, leaning over a set of maps. Arms locked and triceps bulging against the thin cotton cloth of his shirt.

"Amir, you know my answer already," the man said, his voice pitched low and gravelly. "Marcus has urged a war for more than a century now, and we've always been able to avoid it. We'll do it again."

A Nordic-looking man slammed his open palm onto the table then gestured to her. "But if what the seer says is true, we'll all burn in our beds if we don't defend ourselves."

"Even so," the leader said in a more patient voice. "Even if she says the truth, we can't risk our entire species by engaging with him. If the Blackwings get their war, half of the world could burn, and we would annihilate each other. There would be nothing left to protect, and our way of life would be through. We would be nothing but ash and dust. We move our females and offspring into hiding and try to negotiate."

"You can't put off the war forever," the Nordic man said, his voice shaking in anger.

"If any of us want to live, I have to."

Seven men filed out of the room, murmuring their discontent, while the dark-haired man in the middle stood still with his back to her.

Muttering a curse, he sagged against his locked arms on the table and shook his head.

She loved him. She didn't want him to hurt like this. She needed to touch him and reassure him everything would work out, just as it had for centuries. She stood and padded toward him, then reached her pale hand out to touch his shoulder. "My love?"

Clara gasped and sat up, then hunched into herself and grabbed her head to keep it from exploding. Tears streamed from the corners of her eyes, and she gripped her hair in desperation to find relief. Slamming her face into the pillow, she bit the material and screamed into it, her hoarse voice agonized and muffled.

As the stabbing sensation eased from her head and she could see and think clearly again, she sat up and drew her knees up to her chest like a shield to protect her from the awful feeling that had come from that dream.

She hadn't been worried about the war, or the Blackwings, though the name alone had brought on chills. The only feeling that remained was a stark and empty yearning. She missed the man she'd almost touched so deeply her heart felt as if it was being ripped from her chest. She adored and pined for the man in her dreams, and she knew now she was losing her mind.

This was the first dream that had ever made sense, and that was exactly how Grandma's madness had begun.

SIX

Clara couldn't stop her hands from shaking as she made her way down the hallway in search of the kitchen. Without the smell of bacon as her beacon, she would've got lost six turns ago. She clutched the crumpled contract even harder as she turned the corner and saw Damon standing over a stove and cooking scrambled eggs.

"Good morning," he said in a dead tone without turning around.

"I've decided I'll have your baby."

Damon spun around, his eyes wide and shocked. "Excuse me?"

"My answer is yes, but I have negotiations to your contract."

He stood there frozen, egg-covered spatula in hand and his mouth hanging open. He was wearing only a pair of thin, baby blue pajama pants and no shirt. Clara pursed her lips, determined to hold his gaze, but holy shit, her eyes had a mind of their own, and now she was ogling his sculpted torso. Wide, cut shoulders and a straight, deep indentation between his pecs, drawn up nipples and eight perfect abs, flexing with every breath. And oh, the shadows adorned his torso well. He even had those defined muscles over his hips that she found so bitable. But the skin over his muscular physique wasn't smooth as she'd imagined it to be. Instead, it was rough and uneven and darker on some parts than others. Scars, or perhaps old burns? *Shit, stop staring.*

A pungent scent hit her nostrils. "Your eggs are burning."

"What?"

"Your eggs."

"Shit!" Damon spun and yanked the pan off the overkill eight-burner stove. It was deeply satisfying to hear the man curse like a commoner.

With a dragon growl that rattled the room, he gritted his teeth until a muscle in his chiseled jaw bulged. He glared at the ruined food. "Everything else is ready, but you'll have to wait on the eggs," he muttered as he pulled a carton out of the fridge.

Clara looked around at the plates overflowing with pancakes, waffles, French toast, bacon, sausage, biscuits, and cinnamon rolls. "I think we will be okay without the eggs."

"I eat a lot," he said low, eyes narrowed on hers. "I'm going to go put on a shirt."

Right. She was staring again. "No, don't! I mean," Clara said, lowering her voice to a non-lunatic volume. "I like the way you look like this, all disheveled and natural. It makes you less intimidating."

He sighed out a troubled sound and crossed his arms over his chest. "I'm not saying I agree to this, but tell me your negotiations while I make you a plate. I'm curious."

"Okay," she drawled out, taking a seat on one of the wooden stools under the kitchen island. The room matched the hallway. White, sterile cabinets to match white marble countertops. It made her want to pull a hoodie on. "First off, I should tell you why I'm agreeing to this so you understand where I'm coming from. I'm not in this for the money, and I don't need you to take care of me like that. I mean, a little support wouldn't hurt, but I don't need you providing for me. I can take care of myself and…our…baby."

Damon looked troubled as he loaded pancakes onto her plate, but nodded. "Go on."

"I liked the way you were with Rowan last night, and it's nice to imagine you caring for our… God, this is weird. It's weird talking about this, right?" Clara shook her head. "Moving on. I've wanted a baby for a long time. And I don't know how much of a background check you did on me, but I had a crew once. I had two males under me, and I loved them."

"Both of them?"

"Yes, but not in the way you're thinking. They were my best friends. We did everything together, and we were deliriously happy." She licked her lips and swallowed hard at the memory of the day her dreams had been crushed.

"Don't say anymore," Damon said suddenly, and when she looked up, she could've sworn there was fear in his dark eyes. "I don't want to hear the rest. I already know. I read it."

Hurt, jagged and red, washed through her. Steeling herself, she whispered, "Fine. I wanted a baby, and they wanted to help me raise one, so we tried."

"With both?"

Clara nodded. "It wasn't gross or strange to us, but before it happened...well... you read the rest."

Damon looked sick as he slid her plate toward her. He turned his back on her and began cracking eggs into a bowl. "Continue."

"I was empty after— Fuck." Clara scraped her teeth against her lip in an effort to keep her emotions in check and said, "Anyway, I went to the doctors and did everything like I was supposed to until I ran out of money." Tears blurred her vision at how big a failure she'd been. "One baby took, but it didn't keep," she whispered. "I've never told anyone that before."

Damon's shoulders were rigid as he worked stiffly over the stove, and he banged the pan onto the back burner so hard, the sound made her jump. He hooked his hands on his hips and stared out the window, his back a stony silhouette in the early morning light. Without a word, he turned and strode around the island, his eyes blazing in the instant before he crushed her to his chest. Shocked, she froze as his skin burned against hers. And when her surprise wore off, she slowly lifted her hands and hugged him, running her palms over his uneven skin.

"I'm sorry," he said. "Sorry that happened. Sorry you lost…" He huffed an exhalation and gripped the back of her wild hair, burying his face against her neck. "Fuck, you smell good. Soap and fruit and mint."

"I brushed my teeth," she muttered like a sexpot. Real smooth.

He rattled a satisfied-sounding rumble as he sidled closer between her legs until he pressed against her sex. Clara cursed how thick the denim material of her jeans were. "Negotiation number one," she whispered, running her fingernails up and down his back. "No more doctors. And no ovulation tests or worrying obsessively over whether it will happen for us."

"What do you mean, no doctors?"

"Your contract says you want to get me pregnant with doctors, but I don't want this to be scientific. I tried that, and it was a cold and lonely experience. I want to do this the old-fashioned way."

Damon was still breathing against her skin, and now he plucked at her neck gently with his lips. Her sex throbbed once, the little beggar.

"You want me to breed you the old-fashioned way then?"

"Negotiation number two, stop using the words breed or breeder. It's sex, and we're friends with benefits who share a common goal of making a baby. Together."

"Sex," he murmured in an odd, animalistic voice she didn't recognize.

Oh, he smelled good, too. Soap and man and syrup with a hint of smoke. How was his skin so hot? *Focus.*

"Th-three. I want to co-parent. I know male dragons usually raise the kids, but I want in on this, too. I want the whole experience. I don't just want to be pregnant, Damon. I want to be a mother. If we're successful, I'll move to Saratoga, and we'll do this thing together."

"What else?" Damon asked, grazing his teeth against her neck.

She couldn't think with his teeth on her like this. Bitey dragon was going to make her come without even touching inside her panties.

"Four," she said, forcing herself to lean back. Clara cupped his cheeks and brought his fevered gaze to hers. "You can't be disappointed in me if it doesn't happen, and you can't be disappointed if the baby turns out to be a grizzly like me."

Damon's gaze was lightening by the

second to that silver that churned like storm clouds. He looked down at her lips and blinked slowly. "Anything else?"

"I'm not signing this contract. We're ripping it up and doing this as friends, not business partners. You don't owe me some cushy comfortable life after all is said and done. I wouldn't feel right taking your money past what you want to help out with the baby. Deal?"

Damon dragged his attention back to her eyes and angled his head thoughtfully. "No contract?"

Clara grabbed a knife from the crystal butter dish and cut a slit across her palm, then turned his hand over and did the same to his. While hers dripped red and filled the air with the scent of iron, Damon's cut healed instantly, only offering a small line of blood no bigger than a papercut.

His voice was hollow when he murmured, "I don't bleed much."

Offering her hand for a shake, she said, "No matter. It's enough. Shake to seal the deal."

He pressed his palm against hers and that same shocking pain she'd felt last night when she'd touched him for the first time zinged up her nerve endings.

"Ouch," she yelped, yanking her hand back. She looked at the stinging cut and gasped as it glowed orange from the inside and healed instantly. Her bear shifter healing was fast, but not that efficient. "What the hell?" she asked on a shocked breath.

Damon frowned at her hand as he rubbed his own. He said something so softly, even with her impeccable hearing, she almost missed it. She could've sworn it sounded like, "Dangerous Clara."

With a sharp inhalation of breath, he drew her knuckles to his lips and let his mouth linger against her skin. "I accept your negotiations. We can start trying whenever you like."

"Hmm," she hummed as she leaned forward and kissed his throat. "I'll have to check my schedule, but I might be able to pencil you in now."

"Now?" he asked as he angled his head back and gave her more access to nibble at his neck. His shoulders shook curiously, as if she'd given him chills.

"Unless you want to enjoy your pancakes first."

Damon dropped his chin to his chest and smiled at the plates of food, and for a moment, she thought he was going to choose breakfast over her. But then he turned just enough that his lips pressed onto hers. His mouth moved against hers easily, like water. She tasted sweet syrup as he pushed his tongue gently past the parted seam of her lips.

A soft moan escaped as she wrapped her arms around his neck and melted against him. Gently, he pulled her to the edge of her stool and harder against his long erection. Holy moly, she was being kissed! This wasn't the passionless pecks from her crew or the empty goodnight kisses she'd had when she'd tried her hand at dating. This was passion and fire burning her up from the middle outward. This was limbs going numb and hearts pounding against each other. This was falling for a man with a touch. Her stomach dipped like she was on a rollercoaster, and she opened her eyes in a rush just to make sure they weren't floating.

Damon eased back and pressed his forehead against hers. His breath shook, and he closed his eyes, hiding the brilliant color from her.

"No, no, Mr. Dragon," she whispered, cupping his cheeks. "Don't hide yourself from me."

Damon's nostrils flared, and his chest rose

and fell with his quick, panting breath. "It's been a while."

"Since what?"

She thought he would say since he'd had sex with a woman, but he shocked her into stillness when he said, "It's been a while since I let anyone in."

Clara's lip trembled, so she bit hard to steady it. "I won't hurt you." And for some reason she couldn't fathom, that was the easiest oath she'd ever made. Damon was fierce and strong. Deadly. But as he lifted those uncertain silver eyes to hers, the ones with the long pupil that contracted as he focused on her face, it was clear that Damon guarded his heart as the dragons of legend had guarded castles and helpless maidens.

She wanted in. Wanted to be close to him more than anything she'd ever wanted in her life. It felt significant and necessary. Whoever she'd been yesterday didn't matter anymore, because when she was around Damon, she felt bigger. She felt important again after losing her self-worth somewhere along the way. Without words, just by looking at her with that vulnerability churning in his mercury-colored eyes, he was offering her a little sliver of his cold heart that he'd warmed just for her. And that ounce of trust he was offering bound her to him. The threads of her soul reached out, desperate to embrace his as he leaned forward again and sipped her lips. The urgency had dimmed from his kiss and been replaced with a timid, silent question. *Am I worthy*?

Her heart was swelling, filling her chest cavity until it was hard to breathe. She ran her fingertips gently through his hair as she angled her head and parted her lips for him. Damon brushed his tongue against hers, and she released a long, shaky sigh, expelling her nervousness completely. She trusted him. It made no sense that she trusted a man like Damon so quickly, but for unexplainable reasons, and more to do with instinct, she did. He was good—not the monster she'd thought. The cold mask he wore was a façade to protect himself from letting people in, but it slipped away around her.

Damon leaned forward and hooked his arm under the backs of her knees, then picked her up. He carried her as a groom carried a bride over the threshold. His gait was easy and unhurried, and he rested his cheek against her hairline as he took her out of the kitchen and down a hallway lit only by an occasional chandelier. There were no windows to allow in natural sunlight, and the farther he walked, the darker and colder it became.

He hadn't shaved this morning, and the short scruff on his jaw scratched against her forehead as he took a right down another hallway, this one even darker than the last. Here the walls were illuminated by old-fashioned candle lanterns that lifted the hairs on the back of her neck with familiarity.

"Are you taking me to your lair?" she asked quietly, as if the volume of her voice would ruin the magic of this moment.

"I am, fair maiden. Do you oppose?"

She smiled at his formal words with their edge of teasing. Perhaps others didn't understand Damon's subtle humor, but she did. She smiled up at him and shook her head. "Nae, savage dragon. Take me to your lair with haste, for I oppose you not."

The glow of the candle lanterns threw shadows across his face, making his eyes look stark in contrast. She should be scared with him looking so fierce and otherworldly, but all she could think right now was how strikingly handsome he was.

She brushed her fingertip across his cheek, just under the blazing color. His long pupils contracted and dilated between lanterns, and she smiled proudly at him. "*My* dragon," she murmured.

"Not even bedded yet and already possessive." His lips lifted at the corners and gave her a brief view of those dimples she was beginning to breathe for.

Damon angled his body and pushed against a towering, ancient wooden door. Inside, he set her on her feet and eased back by inches, inhuman eyes intent on her.

It was dark in here, and she had to wait for her eyes to adjust, but when they did, she was stunned. She stepped forward into the cavernous room. It was enormous and carved into the cliff. Behind a huge bed was nothing but a dark, dripping, jagged rock face. Two sides of the room seemed to be made of blackout panels that had been lowered to block out the sunlight. He didn't move to open them though, and it struck her that he cared what she thought of his lair the way it was. Cold with a constant *drip drip* sound coming from the far wall. For how big the room was, there was very little furniture, and the floor under her bare feet was made of cobblestone.

"I know it's not as warm as a bear's den. It's probably unnaturally uncomfortable to you," Damon said low, his eyes still trained on her.

She shook her head. "I've never seen any place like this," she said. Her words echoed through the room and bounced back to them. She grinned and called, "Hellooooo!" *Hellooo, hellooo, hellooo.* "You want to know my favorite part about this room?" she asked excitedly.

"Yes. Tell me."

"You didn't make your bed."

He huffed a surprised laugh and ran a hand through his sleep mussed hair. He cast the unmade bed a self-deprecating look and shook his head. "Mason is the only one who has ever been in here, so there doesn't feel like a need to waste the energy on making it."

"I don't make my bed either. Do you want to know my second favorite part about this room?"

He dipped his chin once, his eyes going serious.

"I like that besides you, only Mason has seen it."

"And now you."

She canted her head and smiled. "Exactly."

"Possessive," he accused.

"Slob," she retorted.

His smile lifted and fell. "Sexy," he rumbled

low, stalking her as she backed playfully toward the bed.

When the backs of her legs hit the carved wooden footboard, she folded onto the plush mattress behind her, never taking her gaze from his as he approached. He was all silver eyes and flexing muscles with every lithe step he took. Even with his uneven, scarred skin, Damon was beautiful in ways that made her heart stutter. "Mine," she whispered.

His lips crashed onto hers as he hovered over her, keeping his body weight from pressing her into the comforter. Her legs spread for him instinctively, just to give him room to settle against the apex between her thighs. Rolling his hips, Damon pressed his erection right at the spot she was most sensitive. Arching her back against how good he felt right there, she offered him her neck, something she'd never done for another man.

A satisfied rumble vibrated from Damon's chest and made a quick *puh, puh, puh* sensation against her skin. "Fearsome grizzly, offering your submission so soon." Damon leaned forward and clamped his teeth onto her neck, hard enough to draw a moan from her lips, but not hard enough to break the skin. He released her and murmured against the base of her throat, "No need to submit to me, love. I like you how you are."

Love. The way he uttered that word dumped heat between her legs. She wanted to feel the burn of his hot skin against hers. As if he could read her thoughts, he pulled the hem of her shirt upward and over her head in one smooth motion, then unsnapped the back clasp of her bra with an easy *snick*. With one finger, he hooked the front of her open bra and pulled it from her arms. He blinked slowly as he dropped her undergarment off the edge of the bed, then dragged his gaze back to her bare breasts. Now the insecurity set in. Damon had lived for eons and had likely been with countless women over the course of his existence, while she was a novice who, at age thirty, had only managed to sleep with one college boyfriend and her crew mates. And none of those times had she encouraged them to look at her body.

"You're beautiful."

"I'm freckled."

"I'm scarred. Does it make you want me less?"

She shook her head and answered honestly, "I think it makes me want you more."

Damon leaned forward and sucked gently

on her earlobe, then whispered, "I like your spots." Easing back, he traced a constellation of them over the tip of her shoulder.

Nervously, she said, "You must have very good vision in the dark."

"Impeccable vision."

"Faaantastic."

Damon angled his head, and his eyes narrowed slightly. "Can you not feel how hard I am between your legs, Dangerous Clara? Can you not feel how badly I want you? How badly I want to be inside of you." He leaned down, drew one of her nipples into his mouth, and grazed his teeth against the sensitive skin there as though he was punishing her. "I've never seen a woman so beautiful. Now," he murmured, rolling her on top of him until her legs straddled his hips, "own me."

Eep! Own him? She was more of a wiggle around on the bottom and hope for an orgasm type of gal, but Damon—sexy, dominant, apex legendary predator, Damon—was handing her the reins in his bed. "I don't think I'll be very good at this." Where the hell had her confidence run off to?

Damon grabbed a pillow from above him and fluffed it under his neck, then linked his hands behind his head. With a crooked, cocky smile, he said, "Take my pants off."

Right. She could do that. *Look sexy*. She scraped her nails down his hips as she fumbled with the elastic band of his thin pants. He tensed under her and made an inhuman hissing sound. She thought she'd hurt him, but when she muttered, "Shit," and looked up to apologize for what a horrid seductress she was being, his eyes were narrowed to hungry slits and his smile turned positively wicked.

"Do that again."

Mmm, the dragon liked her claws. Eyes on his face, Clara grabbed the elastic on either side of his hips and dragged it slowly down his thighs, clawing him gently as she unsheathed him. Damon shivered, and under her touch, gooseflesh raised from his skin. The breath she exhaled was still shaky, but her hands had stopped trembling. His skin was like hot tap water that was almost uncomfortable to touch but still bearable. She liked that he ran hot. Finding her bravery, she looked down at his long, thick shaft. It was red and swollen, ready for her, and already a drop of creamy moisture sat on the tip. She smiled and bent down to taste it before she could change her mind. The second she touched her mouth to his dick, his hands went to her hair, gripping her gently as he drew a knee up on one side of her and let off a soft, helpless groan. Holy sexy balls, he was hot. Damon curled his hips forward as she slid her mouth over him. She thought he would shove her where he wanted with a grip as strong as his, but he didn't. He kept his hands gentle in her hair, guiding but not forcing. She eased off him, then back down, circling him with her tongue.

"Fuuuck," he gritted out as she took more of him. His abs flexed every time she slid her mouth over him, and relaxed when she pulled slowly off.

She wasn't scared about what he would think anymore or insecure about the way she looked. Now, she was molten in her middle, and her want for him outshone any hesitation.

She unsnapped the button to her jeans and ripped the zipper slowly down.

"Touch yourself," he whispered as he watched her shimmy out of the rest of her clothes.

Feeling like a goddess under his intense gaze, Clara straddled her knees on either side of his hips and locked her arm near his ribs. She rocked forward, arching her back as she ran her hand between her breasts and down the center of her stomach, lower and lower until she touched the top of her sex.

"More," he said, voice sounding breathless now as he wrapped his fist around his shaft and drew a long stroke.

She cupped herself gently. "Like this?"

He nodded jerkily and pulled another stroke of himself. "What do you feel?"

"Wet."

Damon moved so fast, he was a blur. Her stomach dipped as she went from hovering over Damon to under his body on the bed. Breath quick and shallow, he pressed her knees apart with his own and curved his powerful hips against hers. His shaft slid into her by inches, and she gasped at how good he felt inside of her, stretching her. He drew out and bucked into her again, deeper this time. Clara clawed his back and bowed against the bed. "More," she demanded, using his own word.

A long, low rumble filled the room and rattled against her skin as Damon plunged into her so deeply, he pressed onto her clit. She moaned his name and clutched onto him tighter as he eased out and thrust into her again.

"Fuck, how can you feel so good?" he asked breathily. His lips collided with hers as he thrust into her again.

God, he was big. If she hadn't been so ready for him, this would've toed the edge of discomfort, but right now, all she could do was close her eyes and absorb every sparking sensation that exploded in her middle every time he buried himself inside her.

The pressure between her legs was so intense she gripped the back of his hair and raked her fingernails across his back to anchor herself in the here and now. She was at risk of floating away. Of losing herself and not retaining the clean-edged memories of this moment. And she wanted to remember everything because this, right now, felt important. It felt all-encompassing, as though her life was taking an unexpected fork in the road, and at the edge of her path would be a cache of wealth so much more valuable than riches. Happiness lay in front of her now.

Damon's grip at the base of her neck tightened as he kissed her and thrust into her hard, faster now. His control was slipping, and damn she loved this. Loved to hear that prehistoric growl in his throat. Loved to feel his hands tightening against her skin. Loved to feel him swelling even bigger inside of her. She was close. So close.

As if Damon could feel her tipping over the edge, he grabbed her wrists and slammed them down against the bed above her. He lifted his torso and stared down at her, watching her face as her body exploded around him. "Damon!" she screamed, arching her neck back as her body pulsed with pleasure.

A snarl lifted his lip as he closed his eyes and slammed into her, then froze. Jets of warmth throbbed into her, and he bucked erratically as he uttered her name through clenched teeth. "Clara." And as he emptied himself into her completely, he lowered himself flush against her, hard chest against her soft breasts, and he bit her exposed neck again. Just a clamp of his teeth as her aftershocks pulsed on, and then he replaced the sharp edges with soft kisses.

And when her body had gone still and sated, he eased out of her and pulled her close against his chest. His skin was warm against hers, but it felt good here in the cold cavern of his lair.

He let his lips linger on her forehead and he rubbed her back gently over and over, as if he was helpless to stop touching her now.

Clara smiled against his skin.

Own me.

Damon had it all wrong.

He was the one who owned her now, body and soul.

SEVEN

"I want pancakes," Clara said. "I want to be able to tell everyone I was fed by a dragon."

"As opposed to being fed *to* a dragon?" Damon asked with a deep chuckle that reverberated under her cheek. He was lying comfortably on his back, tugging at her wild curls as she rested her face against his chest. She was actually getting used to Damon's heat now, and even the darkness of his lair. It was nice in here, sequestered away from the rest of the world. It could be burning to the ground for all she knew, but in here, she was safe and warm and Damon's.

She traced his uneven skin around a darker scar. "What happened to you?"

His nostrils flared as he inhaled deeply. "War. I'll be right back."

He eased out from under her and off the

bed, then sauntered to a single door she hadn't noticed before. When he turned on the light inside the room, she could see rows of suits and clean-pressed shirts lined up. As he began to dress, she pulled the covers over her body to make up for Damon's lost warmth.

War. Something about his flippant response niggled at her mind, as if a memory was clicking into place that she didn't understand or realize quite yet. Unsettled, she watched him stride toward the door as he buttoned up a starched, white shirt over dark gray dress pants. Damn, the man could wear a suit, but his passive mask was secured back onto his face. She hated seeing the look of indifference after the last hour they'd shared.

"Damon?"

He turned at the door, but hesitated to meet her eyes. She wanted to tell him how much being with him here had meant to her. She wanted to tell him how hard she was falling for him, and how much she appreciated him letting her in, even if it was just for a little while. His dead gaze made her cowardly though, so instead, she murmured, "You have a file on me. Can I see it?"

"Why?" he asked, not even bothering to deny it.

She gathered the pillow more securely under her head and admitted, "I'm curious about what made Mason decide to bring me here."

Seconds of silence ticked on between them before Damon dipped his chin once. "As you wish."

After he left, Clara debated getting dressed, but decided against it. She'd been comfortable in her own skin with him and wanted that feeling back. He'd seemed completely content to lie with her for hours until she'd asked him about his past. About his scars. He might have let her in a little, but Damon was far from an open book and would likely always be that way. Something about that made her chest ache.

He wasn't gone more than ten minutes and returned with a tray stacked high with food and a beige file dangling from his hand. He kicked the door closed behind him and set his wares on the bed.

"Will you undress again?" she asked, as he hesitated by the bedside.

He shook his head slowly and sat on the edge of the mattress, his now dark gaze on her.

"Is it because I asked about your scars?"

A single nod, and then he stared off at the

door as if he wanted to escape her. "It's best not to scratch at me, Dangerous Clara. Those ghosts you are able to see so easily are better left alone."

Clara looked around the room at the mention of them, but it was only her and Damon here now. "I'm sorry."

Damon looked troubled, but rewarded her with unbuttoning his shirt and yanking the material off his shoulders. The pants stayed in place, but at least she had access to his warm torso again as he settled against the headboard beside her. Tray between them, they ate in silence, and when she'd had her fill, she pulled the file into her lap.

Damon picked up a remote from the end table near the bed and pushed a button that lifted one of the blackout panels. She gasped at the view. His room was overlooking the beautiful evergreen forest. Blinking hard at what a turn her life had taken in the last few days, she squinted against the saturated sunlight filtering through the wall-to-ceiling window.

She read her file out loud. "Clara Emory Sutterfield. Birthdate, ten twenty of nineteen eighty five. Grizzly lineage…" her voice trailed off.

"Read on."

"Grizzly lineage began six generations ago." She hadn't even known when her family had gone bear shifter. "Green eyes, red hair, five-foot-five, curvy figure." Here someone had scribbled, *this one feels important.* She looked at Damon and quirked her eyebrows.

He shook his head and muttered, "That is Mason's writing."

Huh. She continued. "One red-headed female born to each generation. Dominant grizzly shifter. Alpha of the Red Claws. Lost..." Her voice faded to nothing. She shouldn't have asked to see this. It was nothing she didn't already know. She'd lived it. Barely survived this part, in fact. Her voice shook as she read on. "Lost her crew, Charles Redding and Daniel Myer, to an explosion on an offshore drilling rig. Didn't recover." She huffed a sad and humorless laugh. *Didn't recover.* Her or her crew? Didn't matter. It was true on both accounts.

"Why didn't you find another crew?" Damon asked low. He wouldn't look at her anymore. His attention was on a loose thread on the comforter that he wrapped around and around his finger.

Clara lifted one shoulder in a helpless

shrug. "I just couldn't love anyone like that again."

"Because you were afraid to lose them?"

Her lip trembled, and her vision blurred with tears. Blinking hard, she nodded her head. She couldn't trust her words right now. She couldn't trust her words about her crew ever. Burying them had broken all the good things she'd liked about herself. She'd lived a half-life ever since. Her choice.

"Is the hole they left why you want a child?"

"No," she rasped through a tightening throat. "I wanted a baby before Charles and Daniel died. We had all these plans. We didn't even want to know who the father was between the two of them because we would all be a family, raising our cub, and it wouldn't matter. And then when I…" Her voice broke, so she cleared her throat and tried again. "When I got the call about the accident, all of our dreams of having a family were gone. Just,"—she snapped her fingers—"gone like that. Everything was gone. And after a few years of living this empty, lonely life, I wanted to feel again. I wanted to love someone, but in a safe way, you know? I wanted to be a mother as badly as I ever had, but I'd missed out on bonding to another male after I lost Charles and Daniel. So I tried the doctor's way until my savings ran out. Pretty pathetic, huh?"

Damon sighed and draped his arm over her shoulders, then pulled her tight against his side. Turning his head, he rested his chin on top of her hair. "I would've done the same thing."

Clara's shoulders sagged, and a sob worked its way up her throat. "It feels good to say all that out loud and not carry it alone anymore."

"Dangerous Clara," he said softly.

He'd called her that several times now, and she winced against the moniker. She wanted to tell him he was wrong, and that she wasn't dangerous to him at all. She wanted to tell him to stop calling her that and go back to calling her *love* as he had earlier. She wanted to tell him he was wrong about her, and that she would never hurt him, but when she opened her mouth to explain all of this, the words stuck in her throat. Why? Because she suddenly understood him.

I would've done the same thing, he'd said.

He had done the same thing.

Something in his past had brought him to his knees and made it easy for him to shut down his emotions. To turn his face into a lineless, emotionless mask.

He didn't want her talking about his past or breaking down his walls, and she understood his hesitation. She was terrified of him for the same reasons.

The life of a fearful grizzly had clashed with that of a stone-cold dragon, and somehow along the way, they'd become one in the same.

He could call her "Dangerous Clara" all he wanted to. Because now, she'd opened up her heart to him and given him the ability to hurt her.

Now, he was Dangerous Damon.

EIGHT

Pain, jagged like broken glass, sliced through her head.

Clara buckled into herself with a whimper as a screaming sound pounded against her ears. She convulsed, then opened her eyes as the ache behind them lessened. That steady current of sound wasn't screaming at all. It was the wind.

Looking down, she had to be a mile above the ground. She wanted to gasp, wanted to panic. Wanted to scream, but she couldn't do anything other than observe.

This was a dream. One of those nightmares that felt so real, like the ones Grandma used to have. A wave of sorrow washed over her as she thought about how fast the insanity was happening. She'd wanted to experience motherhood before she went. She wanted to raise a child before the end of her life. Before the end of her clarity. Selfish.

She couldn't speak and couldn't move, but beside her, something enormous beat the air currents. Wings the color of fire flapped on either side of her, and when she looked down, four giant red claws were tucked close to her cream-colored belly scales.

She was a dragon.

Below, rocky crags and wilderness stretched as far as she could see. There weren't homes or farmland or landing strips. The world was just...empty.

A deafening roar sounded from her throat as she tucked her wings and dove for the trees. Faster and faster she fell, and just as she thought she would hit the ground, a clicking sounded in her throat and she opened her mouth, releasing hellfire onto a clearing. She scooped up the burning ash, swallowed it down, and immediately she felt energized. Flapping her wings, she angled herself toward the setting sun and pushed her body harder, faster. The sense of urgency never left until she stretched her claws out and lowered herself to the ledge of a cliff face.

He was there waiting, her Damon, but his face was haggard. His eyes were dull and the color of pitch, tired and worried, and he looked as though he hadn't slept in days.

"What are you doing here?" he asked in that strange language.

Her claws hit the rock, and she shattered inward, shrinking until she was on two bare feet again. Agony ripped at her heart because she was about to break his.

"I had to see you one last time."

"One last time? What are you talking about?"

"Damon, he knows. Marcus knows about us, and he's threatened to never rest until you and all of your clan are charred and dead."

"Feyadine, how did he find out about us?" His voice cracked with power as he glared at her.

"Because I uttered your name," she admitted, cheeks burning with shame.

He'd told her once, "I'll love you always."

She'd told him then, and she meant it, "You won't. You can't. You love me now only because you haven't seen the monster I am yet." Now he would see her for how weak she really was.

"You uttered my name?" he said low, suspicion filling his eyes and sparking them to the bright silver color she was used to. "When, Feyadine?"

"When I was with him."

Damon shook his head and backed away a step, and then another, the betrayal in his eyes like a lash against her soul.

"I've been his all along. It wasn't my choice—"

"No."

"Listen to me, please," she said, sobbing as warm tears trailed down her face. Monster, monster, monster. "I didn't choose him, Damon. You have to believe me."

"Yet you've visited my bed all this time. You've endangered my people. You've endangered me!"

"I am a Blackwing! What can I do other than to obey Marcus's rule?"

"You're a fucking fire-breather, Feyadine! A powerful seer and a fire-breather and you can't convince me that the choice wasn't yours. You aren't some weak female."

"I'm pregnant!"

Damon drew back as if he'd been slapped. His face crumpled, and he shook his head in denial. "No, Feya. No. You have another century before you're ready to bear offspring. You're too young."

"It's early still, but I'll have to stop Changing soon to protect my offspring. I'm pregnant, Damon, and I don't know if my eggs belong to

you or to…"

"Marcus," he gritted out, eyes blazing. "Did he force you?"

Her voice was nothing but a whispered admission of how utterly she'd failed and betrayed him. "No." She wished her answer was different, but she was the vilest of monsters. "I came to tell you goodbye. It isn't safe to see you anymore. Marcus watches me now, and I don't want him finding you or your people." She wiped her damp cheeks with the back of her hand and tried to hide the depth of her heartbreak. She'd failed her people and herself, but worst of all, she'd failed Damon. He was too good, too caring. He'd fought for hundreds of years to keep his people safe, but the mighty Damon Daye, alpha of the Bloodrunners, had fallen for someone beneath him. He'd fallen for her.

"Was it all a lie?" he asked, voice bleak.

"No. I love you. If I'd had a choice, it would've been you."

Disgusted, he closed his eyes and angled his face away from her. "I never want to see you again."

His words cut through her middle, and she cried out in pain. She wished she could die now. She wished her death wasn't meant for when she would bear offspring she would never see hatch. She wished she could jump off these cliffs and end her suffering. He would be better off if she'd never existed, but that wasn't her fate. Her fate was to fly away from the man she loved and endure the continuing wrath of a mate who had many conquests just like her.

"What if the eggs are yours?"

Damon slid her a dangerous glare. "You're one of the mates of Marcus, Feyadine. Do you think he would let me take offspring from him? You've taken my chance at fathering young with you, no matter if they're mine or not. Your eggs and your death will help build Marcus's army."

"Damon," she said in a broken whisper, tears dripping from her cheeks.

"Leave." He wouldn't look at her anymore, and the muscles in his jaw twitched as he clenched his teeth harder. "I said leave!"

"I'm sorry," she sobbed, then turned and jumped from the cliff. For a moment, she spread her arms and let the wind catch her, but the rocks below wouldn't kill her. Her skin was hard as stone. She Changed and spread her wings at the last moment, then flew away from Damon without a single look behind her.

She couldn't stomach seeing the betrayal

etched into his beautiful face again.
I'll love you always.
You won't.
You can't.

****

The remnants of that awful dream and the headache that had come along with it had Clara stumbling down the hallway. She hadn't meant to fall asleep in Damon's lair, but she'd woken all alone and cold to the *drip drip* of water falling from the stone wall.

The dream had broken her heart.

"Feyadine," Dream Damon had called her. It was the same name Mason had uttered the first time she'd met Damon. The hallways were dark, even when she reached the pristine white marble ones, but Clara knew where he was. She was drawn to him, as if they were tethered with an invisible string. She turned this way and that in a haze until she reached the top of an old stone spiraling staircase that led down to oblivion for all she knew. There was the soft glow of candlelight, or perhaps torchlight, below, and there he waited for her.

The rounded stone wall was cold and unforgiving under her palm as she descended the stairs. When she finally reached the bottom, she froze, unable to comprehend what was before her.

Damon was on his knees in the middle of a cavernous room, staring at a collage of painted canvases, stacked in layers of disarray and covered heavily with dust. Every painting was of the same subject.

Her.

Clara stumbled forward and drew to a halt right beside him, staring in bafflement at the pictures. There were hundreds of them, all of her face. It was slimmer, and her eyes looked more gray than green. Her freckles were lighter, and her hair was perhaps a shade darker, more auburn than fiery red, but they were of her, no doubt.

"Did you paint these?"

"Yes," Damon said, his voice sounding as hollow as a well without water. "Clara, I heard you."

"Heard me what?"

Damon stood beside her and dusted the seat of his dress pants. He turned an angry silver glare on her and said, "I watched you while you slept, and you said, 'I am a Blackwing. What can I do other than to obey Marcus's rule?'" Damon took a slow, dangerous step toward her. "I saw you. You died in my arms. He'd cut your eggs from you and burned you with dragon's fire, and then he left you in front of that cave full of my murdered people so that I could find you on your dying breath. You. Died. Tell me you died, Feyadine!"

"Don't you dare call my by her name," Clara gritted out. "Don't you *dare*. It was a dream. I've been having her memories for years, only I didn't know what they were. They didn't make any sense until I met you. I'm not Feyadine, and I don't answer to Marcus. I am no Blackwing. I'm Clara Sutterfield, alpha of the late Red Claws and proud grizzly shifter. I would never hurt you like she did."

"You have the fucking Blackwing crest tattooed into your shoulder!"

Damon's middle made a clicking sound, and an instant too late, she realized what it was. Damon hunched into himself and exploded into a massive dragon. She stared in horror as his gigantic body filled most of the cavernous room, felling all of those canvases under his shifting weight. His blue scales shimmered in the candlelight. She would've thought him beautiful if she didn't see the danger of his glare. Chest heaving, she raced away from his clawed feet that pounded on the stone floor. Rocks and dust rained down from the ceiling, and a heavy boulder struck her in the shoulder as she struggled to escape. She cried out in pain as she gripped her arm, pinning it to her side to keep it from hurting worse as she ran for the stairs. A wall of fire sprayed in front of her, and she skidded to a stop, barely able to avoid the flames.

A low, menacing rumble filled the room and shook the walls. The paintings around him toppled and fell, but Damon's silver, serpentine eyes were focused on her.

"You. Asshole," she said through clenched teeth. If she was going out in the dungeon of the last immortal dragon, she was going out fighting, and she was going out furred. With a battle scream, she let her raging grizzly have her body. Red fury pounded through her veins as she charged, but Damon had gone still, and the clicking sound in his throat had stopped. With a roar, she leapt at him and clung to his neck, biting and slashing against his stony scales.

The dragon under her claws disappeared like magic, slamming her onto the floor.

Damon stood, human and naked, thirty feet away by the paintings, crouched down with his eyes gone round. He looked so shocked, she would've found it funny if she wasn't about to murder his ass.

She charged again, ignoring the pain from the injury caused by the falling rock. Stupid fucker dragon calling her by another woman's name and then blasting fire at her. He'd singed her!

"Clara, stop. Stop!" Damon yelled, his hands out.

She skidded across the dusty rock floor and came to a sliding halt right before her snout touched his outstretched hands. But just for good measure, she reached out and bit the shit out of his arm. Or at least she meant to bite the shit out of him, but munching on Damon's skin was a lot like taking a bite out of a thick sheet of granite. She was pretty sure she nearly broke a tooth, which pissed her off more.

She bunched her muscles to attack again, but he said, "Clara, I'm sorry."

His unexpected apology and the regret that swam in his eyes drew her up short. Huffing in pain, she took her weight off her bad leg and limped back away from him slowly. With one last lingering look, she turned and made her way toward the stairs. And by the time she'd made her way to the top of the spiral case, she was groaning in pain.

Her shoulder was dislocated and healing out of place. She Changed back in the hallway with a cry of agony and ran for the guest bedroom with her arm clutched to her side.

Stupid man. She was so pissed off at him she couldn't see straight. Couldn't think straight. She rushed down the winding hallways and through the guest bedroom door, where she slammed it as best she could behind her, then made her way into the bathroom and ran the shower water as hot as she could stand it. She needed her muscles as loose as possible if she was going to set her shoulder back into its socket on her own. Stupid, stupid man. And why was she crying? The combination of adrenaline, anger, and pain were making her light-headed.

She pressed her back against the shower wall and slid down, her shoulders shaking with her sobbing.

And then Damon was there, looking at her with his dark eyes gone soft. He stepped into the oversize shower and knelt down beside her. "Shhh," he cooed, wiping her wet tresses from her face. "I'll fix it." He felt her shoulder, dug into the muscle with an expert touch, and snapped it back into place.

She screamed and huddled into herself at

the blast of pain, but he'd done well. The bone was back in its socket, and she could use her arm again. It ached something fierce, but at least it wasn't the blinding, excruciating pain anymore.

Damon sat beside her and dragged her into his lap under the rain shower. "Clara, I'm so sorry. I thought you were her for a minute. I thought I'd been tricked all this time. You said her words in your sleep, and I thought I hadn't remembered her death right. Like maybe she'd lived and was back to torture me again."

"I'm not her. I don't know what is happening to me with the dreams or visions or whatever they are, but I'm me. I'm Clara." She was desperate to hang onto the belief that she wasn't somehow the reincarnation of that woman in the paintings. She didn't want to be Feyadine. Feyadine had betrayed Damon.

"I know you aren't her. I shouldn't have questioned it. I got confused, and I reacted poorly." He rubbed her back, over and over, his touch slick with the hot water. "You're self-assertive and funny. You speak easily with others and can hold my gaze. You're brave and strong. And shit, if you hadn't proven you weren't a dragon by turning into that beautiful grizzly of yours, I would have known you weren't Feyadine by the way you attacked me without hesitation. Feyadine couldn't do any of those things. She was shy and submissive, and it was endearing until she let it turn into weakness instead. You aren't weak, and you aren't anything like her."

"Other than my face."

"My guess is that came along because you are descended from her family's bloodline. Her brother's, in fact. Nall liked mixing with humans and other shifters. He created some of the first dragon hybrids. I've been off balance since the first time I saw you. It feels like something I don't understand is happening, and it's bigger than you, and it's bigger than me. It feels like this storm is churning over our heads and, at any moment, it's going to rain down on us. This can't be fate giving me a second chance at a true mate. Fate doesn't work like that for me. She takes more than she gives. Always has."

"Why do I have her memories, Damon? What's happening to me?"

Damon shook his head and stared at the shower door with a troubled expression as little drops of water fell from the damp ends of his black hair. "I don't know. But we'll figure it out together, okay?"

Clara nodded, but Damon wasn't off the hook yet. "You blew fire at me."

"You bit me, and technically, I didn't blow it at you. I have good aim. I blew it at your exit. I wanted you to Change so I could tell for sure. I had it in my head you would Change into Feyadine's dragon out of fear, but you turned into a pissed off she-grizzly instead."

"Damn straight I was pissed off."

"You were magnificent," he growled out, nipping at her neck. "It was so fucking sexy seeing your animal for the first time. Red hair, red fur. That's where your crew's name came from, isn't it? The Red Claws? And watching you set your angry glare on me and charging to battle at a dead sprint? I'm so damned proud you're mine. If our child turns out to be a bear cub, I hope he's as red-hided as you."

"You still want to have a baby with me?"

Damon chuckled and leaned his head back on the tile wall. "I do."

"Damon?"

"Mmm?"

"You said Marcus cut Feyadine's eggs out of her."

His chest rose and fell in a slow exhalation. "Female full-blooded dragons were different from the hybrid daughters I've had. They lived for a certain amount of time before the instincts to bear offspring became too overwhelming. I thought Feyadine was too young to breed and that I had time with her, but I was wrong."

"What happened?"

"Marcus found my people while I was out scouting a new place to hide them. He killed them all. Women, children, unhatched eggs, all of my warriors. Feyadine's body met me on my return. She hung on long enough for me to say goodbye. She said, 'I'm sorry, and I'll make everything up to you. You won't be alone forever. I'll find you again, and when I do, I'll be stronger. I'll gift you mortality with the blood of an immortal dragon, and you'll be free.' And then she died in my arms."

"What did she mean?"

"Hell if I know. It makes no sense. I'm the only immortal dragon left. I think she was just in so much pain, she didn't know what she was saying." He was quiet for a long time as the water ran down their bodies in rivers. He seemed content to cradle Clara—to just be—but at last, he murmured, "The eggs were mine."

"How do you know?"

"They were blue like my scales, not the

black color of Marcus's dragon. He left them there for me to see." Damon frowned emotionally. "They were so small. He'd broken them all. When you told me about your pregnancy taking but not keeping, I didn't want to talk about it. I didn't want to hear how it hurt you. I don't want you to feel pain like that. I don't want you to feel that emptiness."

"You've lived for a long time, Damon. I could feel it in my dream. The earth was still wild. Did you find more mates?"

"Wives, not mates. Humans. My first three, I buried when they were old and gray, but my fourth took her own life early. She couldn't stand aging while I stayed the same. I didn't look for companionship after that. The other women I found to bear offspring when my dragon craved family were nothing more than business transactions. I couldn't risk getting attached to anyone again. Everyone I've ever known has died, and eventually, it was easier to be alone than to attach to people who disappear in the blink of an eye."

She pressed her lips against the uneven skin on his chest. "That sounds like a shit deal."

Damon snorted. "*Thank* you. I'm pretty sick of everyone thinking I've lucked into living forever. It's not lucky. Immortality is a curse." He plucked at a strand of her damp hair with his lips. "I would give anything to grow old and gray beside you."

"We'd make a fucking hot pair of elderly people."

He laughed a relieved sound, but she needed to know the rest. She needed to know what happened after Feyadine's death before he shut down on her again.

"What happened to Marcus's people? What happened to the Blackwings?"

Damon's lip twitched, and his eyes went cold and dead. "It turns out he had his sites on being the last immortal dragon. He killed all of his own people."

"Oh, my gosh. How could he do such a thing?"

"He fancied himself a god. He wanted to rule the earth without opposition."

"And your scars?"

"Dragon's fire is the only thing that can kill another dragon. I went to war with Marcus to avenge Feyadine and all of our people. I burned him up and left his carcass for the vultures to roost on. I buried my people in these mountains eons ago, and from that day on, this land was mine. These mountains are my treasure. I failed to protect my people, but I've protected their final resting place and will continue to do so until the end of time."

Heart aching, Clara snuggled her cheek against the burn marks on his chest and wrapped her arms around his neck. Damon wasn't some cold, emotionless dragon. He was a man, and a shifter just like her who'd had to find a way to survive something horrific. Something he could never escape. He'd felt everything so deeply for so long, he'd shut down out of self-preservation. Loyal, fearsome, protective dragon. Feyadine had done a number on his heart with her betrayal, and what had happened afterward would've brought other men to their knees. But he'd risen up and gone to war to avenge the people he'd loved.

And now here he was, fighting to protect the land that his people had died on all those centuries ago.

Damon was right that something bigger than both of them was happening, but she wasn't afraid anymore. If he could be so brave for all this time, she could stand strong beside him until they figured out what had caused them to cross paths like this.

She'd respected other men in her life.

She'd been lucky to have time with Charles and Daniel, but what she had with Damon was turning out to be so much different. So much more. For the first time in her life, she knew what it was to love a man.

She wouldn't admit it to him out loud for fear of him shutting down again, but she gave a private smile at what she'd found here in Damon's mountains.

For the first time in a long time, she felt like she belonged.

NINE

Clara shimmied her hips to the sound of the song she had stuck in her head, did a little spin, and plopped a thick slice of provolone cheese onto the sandwich she was making.

Damon had to work today, but he'd told her at breakfast this morning he'd let his chef have some time off so he could cook for her. It still blew her mind that he enjoyed taking care of her so much. She'd been the caregiver in her crew, nurturing Charles and Daniel any time they had a week off of the rig, so the dynamic was so different here. She was repaying Damon's sweet affection and the delicious food he'd been cooking for her by making them lunch—a pair of sandwiches stacked high with meats, cheeses, and vegetables, just like she'd seen on television. Even the bread was fancy and had to be sliced directly from the fragrant loaf.

There had been so many happy, eye-opening moments since their break-down in the shower yesterday, and one of those was that she hadn't had a single headache in an entire day. Not one. And she couldn't get over the giddy sensation that everything was going to be okay. The visions, dreams, coincidences…all of it. Damon was still wary, but she couldn't shake the growing feeling that perhaps the point of all of this was that she and Damon met, and some cosmic unbalance was reset by them finding each other.

She turned around and startled to a stop, dropping a slice of roast beef onto the tile floor with a tiny *splat*.

A striking woman with dark hair, dark eyes, and the smoothest, fairest porcelain skin she'd ever seen stood in the doorway smiling at her. "Hello. Sorry, I didn't mean to startle you." She approached and held out her hand. A little girl followed closely behind, gripping onto her jeans. "I'm Damon's daughter, Diem, and this is my daughter, Harper."

Clara's eyes bulged wide as she hurried to wipe her hands on a napkin to shake Diem's outstretched palm. "Oh, I would've dressed up and done my hair if I knew I was meeting you today. Damon's talked about you." Clara patted her wild hair, which did nothing but fluff it up more.

Diem's grin grew deeper, and her dark eyes danced. "I like that you aren't dressed up. Formal isn't my favorite."

Clara would definitely say she wasn't a formal type of gal. She was wearing frayed cut-off shorts with holes that allowed her upper thighs to play peek-a-boo, and a T-shirt clung to her torso like a second skin. She and Damon were a study in opposites.

"Hi, Harper," she said, kneeling by Diem's legs. She offered her hand for a shake, and the little girl stepped out from behind her mother. She was perhaps four years old, and when Harper lifted a shy gaze to Clara, she stifled a gasp. Dark ringlets of shiny hair tumbled down the sides of her round cheeks, but her eyes were the real stunners. One was a soft brown color, like Diem's, and one was blue with a long, reptilian pupil. "Ooooh, are you a little warrior dragon?" Clara asked low.

The girl smiled and nodded as she gripped her index finger and shook it.

"I *love* dragons."

"What are you?"

"I'm a warrior grizzly."

The little girl smiled bigger. "I *love* grizzlies."

Clara chuckled and jerked her chin toward the counter piled high with food. "Are you hungry? I have all the sandwich stuff out still if you want to help me make one."

"Can I make my own?"

Clara nodded decidedly. "Of course. If your mom says it's okay."

Diem gave her consent, and the little girl blasted off toward the sprawling pantry, only to return moments later with a little red stepstool. "Pop-Pop gave me this so I could help Chef while he's cooking," she explained in a squeaky little voice that made Clara want to scoop her up and cuddle her."

Harper went to work making a sandwich and a mess of the counters, and Clara turned to Diem and asked, "Where did the name Pop-Pop come from?"

"Well, that one," Diem said, leaning on the counter and nodding toward her daughter, "is a fire-breather like Damon. She was a little hellion when she learned she could do it, blowing flames at anyone who told her 'no,' so I sent her up here with Damon for a few weeks last summer, and he got her straightened right out."

"How?"

"Fire with fire, and Harper came back a lot more cognizant that her flames hurt people and that it wasn't okay to throw tantrums like that. Thanks to him warning her off bad behavior with a couple of warning clicks of his firestarter, she now calls him Pop-Pop."

Clara ducked her head, laughing. "Oh gosh, I love that."

"You look just like her," Diem said, though her scrunched up nose and apologetic look said she wished she hadn't. "I'm sorry."

"You saw the paintings of Feyadine?"

Diem nodded once. "I grew up on stories of the dragon wars, but I thought they were all pretend. In my father's bedtime stories, Feyadine was the dragon queen who didn't deserve her crown."

"Okay, it feels so weird when you call Damon Father. We look the same age!"

Diem giggled. "Strange, right? Have you met Creed?"

"Yeah, I met all of his Gray Backs, too."

"He's Damon's grandson, and Rowan is his great-granddaughter."

"Stop it."

"I'm serious. Creed is my—he's my nephew!" Diem had the case of the giggles right along with Clara now.

"Wait, did he tell you why I'm here?"

"No, but I can guess. Did you sign a certain contract?"

"God no, but I saw it. I negotiated everything. And then I ripped it up."

"Good for you."

"We are trying for a baby, though. I hope that's not weird for you."

"It would've been weird for me if you were just a breeder like my mother had been. Father is still working on payroll, but I cut out early just to meet the woman who has him in such a mood."

"What kind of mood?"

"He's smiled and laughed more than I've ever seen him do in the span of a few hours. And he's got his jacket draped over the chair with his shirt sleeves rolled up like a total slouch."

"Ha!" Clara clapped her hand over her mouth to soften her laughter. "You just wait, Diem. I'll have him looking like a right proper slob in no time."

"I heard a rumor," Diem said low, her words dotted with giggles. "You got him to shotgun a beer? Please tell me that's true."

"I totally did!"

"What's shotgunning a beer?" Harper asked from behind a sandwich she'd stacked a wobbly foot high.

"It's the game Uncy Denison is always making the boys play when anyone uses the word 'pivot.'"

"Oh, when they drink out of the bottom?"

"Yeeep," Diem drawled. She turned to Clara with a wink and murmured, "We're raising her up real classy."

"I can see that, and I approve." Clara studied Harper for a moment, then let her curiosity get the best of her. "Damon told me you're a hybrid dragon. But he said dragon females...you know..."

"Don't survive childbirth? We don't. It's not like with the bears who stop Changing into their animals during pregnancy. We have to force ourselves not to shift and grow weaker and weaker. I wouldn't survive carrying a baby to term."

"I grew in Riley's tummy," Harper said matter-of-factly. "I use ta be this big." She squished her finger and thumb together.

"Oh. Maybe I should ask you about all of this some other time, in private."

"No, don't worry about it. We're very open with Harper. Riley was our surrogate. She is human and had Harper without any problems, and through all of that, she became my best friend and Drew's mate. She kind of just came in and fit right in with the rest of the Ashe Crew, and now life is unimaginable without her."

"I get to spend the night with Riley and Drew and their new baby on Friday nights so daddy can take mommy to the movies. I give baby Bethany bottles and help Riley change her diapers." The mayonnaise she was squirting on top of her towering sandwich made a farting sound. "She has big, smeary poops sometimes."

"Nice," Clara said.

"So, I was kind of nervous about meeting you, and now I super like you," Diem admitted. She pulled a cell phone from her back pocket. "What's your number? The crews hang out, sometimes for barbecues, sometimes down at Sammy's Bar in Saratoga. We celebrate birthdays and holidays and all that. Usually, Father declines invitations, but I have a feeling you'll be shaking things up around here. I'm going to call you with the invites from here on out if that's okay."

"Uuum, I would love that. Please do. I had so much fun meeting the Gray Backs the other night."

"Oh, God, I don't doubt it. Willa's a hoot."

Clara recited her number for Diem and helped Harper hold her sandwich steady as the little girl balanced the plate and strode unsteadily toward a round dining table off the kitchen.

When the little girl was settled, Clara finished arranging the tray of lunch for her and Damon and said her goodbyes to Diem and Harper. But just as she was about to leave the kitchen, Diem said, "Clara?"

"Hmm?" she asked, turning with the tray balanced in her hands.

"Whatever you're doing with my father?" Diem smiled emotionally. "Keep it up. I haven't ever seen him this happy."

Clara's throat clogged with emotion, and her eyes prickled and blurred. "I will. He makes me happy, too."

She had to gather her wits and settle her emotions as she walked down the halls toward Damon's office. If she was being honest, she'd been nervous about meeting Damon's family, too, but that had gone better than she could've imagined. Diem was easy to talk to and already felt like a friend. And little Harper was sharp as a tack. No doubt in her mind, she would grow up to be a strong dragon female like her mother and definitely not mousey like Feyadine had been.

In a daze, she meandered in through the office door and nearly melted under Damon's greeting smile. His sleeves were rolled up to reveal his muscular, sexy, burn-scarred forearms, and his top button was undone at his throat. And there were those dimples she adored.

"There she is," he rumbled as he set his pen down and leaned back in his leather office chair, hands linked behind his head.

"I brought you lunch," she said unnecessarily, as if he couldn't see the sandwiches stacked to her chin.

"Good, I'm starving."

"You're always starving."

"I have a big machine to feed."

"Yeah, about that. I heard from the Gray Backs you've eaten their enemies."

Damon's smile lingered as he shrugged unapologetically. "No one messes with my mountains."

"And the crews are a part of these mountains now, aren't they?"

The smile dipped from his lips. "They feel like a part of me."

"Cold dragon," she murmured, lifting her chin high. "Warmed to the core by a bunch of rowdy lumberjack werebears. Out of curiosity," she asked, setting one of the giant sandwiches onto the space he was clearing on his desk. "Does it bother you that Rowan and Harper are being raised in trailer parks?"

"Not at all. Their lives are richer for their living situations. They have crews that have linked up like bonded families. They live at the center of the most lethal predator shifters in the world, who would die protecting them, and they are being raised by crews who love them unconditionally. I'm proud of Diem and of Creed for building a life like that for their children. I'd rather them live in the Asheland Mobile Park and the Grayland Mobile Park than here. I raised Diem here, and her life lacked…warmth. It's something I regret."

Pride filled her that Damon wasn't just some rich billionaire dragon pulling the strings of his family like they were his puppets. This man wanted full lives for the people he loved. She respected him more for his answer.

"I met Diem and Harper in the kitchen."

"I knew they weren't cutting out early on payroll day without a reason. I figured they were off to track you down. Diem was very curious about you."

"I like them indescribably much. Diem got my number." She lifted her shoulders to her ears happily. "I'm making friends."

Damon looked genuinely happy as he gestured her to him. She sidled around the desk and sank into his lap. A giggle escaped her lips as he nipped at her neck, just under her ear.

"I knew you would fit in here. You have a warm personality. You weren't meant to be alone, Clara."

"I don't feel alone anymore."

"Mmm," he said, more rumble than word. "Stay with me." His words came out rushed, and when she tried to ease away from his affection to look him in the eyes, he held her tighter in a hug against him. "Stay with me," he repeated slower and lower.

"Of course, I will. We're trying for a baby, remember?"

"No, I mean after that. I had this awful thought yesterday in the shower. I know it's wrong, but for a split second, I thought, I hope it takes us a long time to get pregnant."

"Damon, don't put that into the universe."

"I know. I know it's bad. But I know you'll

move to Saratoga with the baby, and I don't want you to go. I know this is fast, but I don't want you to leave me. I want to co-parent with you here."

"Wait, are you asking me to move in?" she asked, shocked to her bones.

"No. Yes. I don't know. I haven't done this before. I just get this..." Another rattling growl vibrated against her skin, and he crushed her to him harder. "I just get this awful feeling when I think about you living in Saratoga away from me."

"Who is possessive now?" she teased.

"Me."

With a frown, she whispered, "Hey." Cupping his cheeks, she lifted his gaze to hers as she eased back. His eyes were silver where they'd been dark just moments ago. "I'm okay. Nothing's going to hurt me or take me away. It's not like with Feyadine, okay?"

Damon searched her eyes, and after a few seconds, the worry that had pooled in his began to fade. He huffed a laugh and rested his forehead against her cheek. "Sorry."

"Well, don't apologize, Dangerous Damon. I like my man a little growly and possessive. And if the offer still stands..."

"If it still stands, what?" he asked, his deep

timbre hopeful.

"Then yes," she whispered through a smile. Your mountains already feel like home somehow, anyway. I still don't want your money, though," she said, trying her best to look severe and likely failing. "I don't want to be some kept woman."

"Does my wealth make you uncomfortable?"

"Hell yes. I've never had two dimes to rub together. I bet there isn't even cheap pesticides on that lettuce on my sandwich. It'll probably taste weird."

Damon chuckled against her throat and pressed his lips there, right where her pulse was pounding.

"Also, I'm never going to wear fancy clothes, so don't even buy them for me. I won't change. I'm always going to stick out in this fancy mansion like a sore thumb."

"Mmm, that's not true, and I don't want to change you, anyway. I like these cheap, threadbare shorts you wear." He ran his hand up her thigh. "You look sexy as hell walking around my lair looking comfortable. Besides, you're much easier to access in these."

"Our lair now, lover, and I *am* comfortable. You should try it. I could go to the grocery store in these duds, or I could take a nap in them. The sky's the limit."

Damon leaned forward and kissed her with a hint of tongue. Oooh, sexy dragon. His mouth moved against hers as he deepened the kiss, and in a smooth motion, he unfolded from his chair with her in his arms and strode around his desk toward the door. Good, he was going to take her somewhere more private because she definitely didn't want to get caught banging while Diem and Harper were in the house. But nope, Damon settled her on her feet and pressed her back against the wooden doors as he locked the deadbolt. Okay then, they would have to be quiet.

Damon bit her bottom lip and unsnapped the button of her shorts, then slid her bottoms down to her ankles, panties and all. He dropped to his knees and demanded in a whisper, "Take your shirt off."

Okie dokie. She yanked her shirt off her head and wiggled out of her bra faster than the snap of a finger, but Damon seemed fine where he was, eye level with her hips. She opened her mouth to ask if something was wrong, but he gripped her legs, leaned forward, and laved his tongue against her sex right at her clit.

"Ooooh," she groaned. *Quiet.* She clamped her teeth on her bottom lip to remind her horny noises to stay where they were.

Damon sucked gently on her sensitive nub, then brushed his tongue against her again. Her knees were numbing now, but as if he knew she was about to go down like a sack of stones, he gripped her knees and held her upright. Clara ran her hands through his hair, and the next time he ran his clever tongue over her clit, she gripped his head in a silent plead for more. That satisfied rumble she adored rattled from his chest and filled the room. *Quiet, quiet.*

Slowly, Damon slipped his tongue inside of her. Clara's eyes rolled closed at the sparking sensation between her thighs. She rested her head back against the door and sighed out a helpless sound. Over and over he plunged inside of her until pulsing pleasure rocketed through her body. The jingle of Damon's belt brought on another wave of excitement, and when he bit her inner thighs gently, once on each, and turned her slowly until she faced the door, she knew he wasn't done with her yet.

"Arch your back, love," he whispered in her ear as he pressed his erection against her back. She did so happily, desperate to feel him inside of her again. God, she adored when he called her "love." Dangerous Damon and Dangerous Clara had no voice here. What they were doing, bonding to each other so seamlessly... This wasn't dangerous. *Love* was right.

Damon wrapped his arm around her middle and nibbled at the back of her ear. Clara's hips rocked as her desperation piqued. The head of his cock pressed into her by an inch, and she pushed backward, hungry for more of him.

Damon chuckled a deep, sexy sound right against her ear. "Are you eager for me, love?"

"Yes. Call me that again."

Without hesitation, he whispered, "Love," against her ear.

Now both of his arms were around her, one around her middle and one massaging her breast in a needy rhythm as he slid into her from behind.

"More," she demanded on a breath.

Damon smiled against her ear and drew back, then slammed into her. And there were his teeth again, right on her shoulder as he thrust into her over and over. His pace picked up, faster, harder, and she was gone now. Floating. Falling. Nothing to hold onto, and she didn't care to stop the stomach-dipping sensation.

When a feral, wanting growl ripped up her throat, Damon reacted immediately, pounding into her harder. And just as the pressure became too much and her body clenched around his in another orgasm, Damon froze behind her, a snarl in his throat, and his teeth sunk deeply into her neck. She gasped and bowed back against him. Pleasure, pain, pleasure, pain, and the scent of iron filled the air. Warmth running down, pooling in the bowl above her collar bone, streaming down between her breasts. Warmth running down her thighs as Damon's jets of hot release became too much for her to hold.

Her body was on fire.

Fire from the overwhelming heat of Damon's body.

Fire from the warmth that churned in her middle as her release pounded through her.

Fire for the man she adored.

"I love you, I love you," she panted out as he ran his tongue over the claiming mark he'd just given her.

"Mate," he whispered against her skin. "I love you, too."

TEN

"Favorite mate," Clara said, holding onto Damon's shoulders piggy-back style.

"You," Damon said easily as he reached forward and pulled open the front door like it weighed nothing. The towering giant barriers groaned as they swung open and creaked as he closed them again.

"No, I mean out of your human mates." Butterflies had been flapping around in her stomach since he'd first called her that this afternoon in his office.

"I haven't called anyone my mate but Feyadine and you, and you've seen me through her memories. What we had wasn't real. At least not to her. The humans I married were just to stop a freefall. I took on a wife when the loneliness got too bad. When the darkness was so thick, I thought I'd become the dark."

"I think Feyadine loved you, Damon," she said softly. "Not to defend her because I hate what she did to you, but I think you meant a lot to her. At least you felt big when I was in that vision. You felt important. She was hurting deeply when she told you about her betrayal."

Damon shook his head, eyes on the cobblestone driveway he strode down. "She felled all of our people with her treachery."

"Yeah, but she couldn't have known that would happen. It felt like she was unhappy to be mated to Marcus and felt unwanted. Unloved. And then she met you, and she wanted to pretend her life was different. I think she was one of many mates to Marcus and wanted something real. You felt real. When I saw you through her…I loved you." Gah, this was all so confusing.

"My answer is still the same and an easy one for me to give. You are my favorite mate. I wish you had been my only."

"For all this time?"

Damon chuckled and released the backs of her knees, settling her on her feet. He turned and cupped her cheeks, then leaned down and kissed her gently. "For all time."

Her cheeks heated with happiness, and she

brushed her nose against his before she pulled away. Dangerous Damon.

He wrapped his big strong hand around hers and led her toward the waterfall tumbling off the cliffs above. From here, she could hear it clear as a bell. The mist as the falls hit the water below smelled like rain, and the silt that was being stirred from the bottom of the river smelled rich and earthy. The sun beamed down in speckles as they ducked under a low-hanging bald cypress branch and into the woods that encased Damon's perfectly manicured lawn. With the pine-needle blanketed forest floor covered in gold pools of sunlight, and rays of dusty light streaming through the canopy to the soundtrack of the roosting birds' song, this place looked like a completely different world. Walking in front, Damon smiled back at her as he led her toward a thin deer trail in the woods. His smile was bright and easy, flashing those gorgeous dimples, and his dark eyes danced when they landed on her. God, she loved him in this moment, more than anything. This incredible man who had survived so much had chosen her. He made her feel special when it was him who was truly one of a kind.

He'd changed out of his business suit and

into a pair of low slung jeans and a dark gray T-shirt that clung to his ripped upper torso and more loosely around his tapered waist. He'd even forgone his usual polished black leather shoes for a pair of flip flops that looked as if he'd actually worn them before. He'd shocked her in the best way. Damon Daye had a casual side, and she bet he had shared it with very few people. She felt like the luckiest that he shared so much of his secret self with her.

Clutching onto his hand tighter, ignoring the slight sting of his heated skin against hers, she followed him toward the sound of the waterfall that was now blocked by the thick pine canopy above them.

"In storybooks, dragons protect treasure. Do you have piles of gold and gemstones buried deep in your mountains, and if so, can you draw me a treasure map? I've always wanted to swim in a pile of gold coins."

He laughed and shook his head. "My treasure is this land. The mountains themselves are what my dragon protects."

Her stomach fluttered at his open admission. She'd only been joking, but he'd gifted her with honesty. She looked around at the mountain peaks surrounding them, covered in evergreens. It was nothing but miles of rolling hills—beautiful, lush, and stoic.

Damon had bound himself to something that could never die. Like him.

With a shake of her head, she said, "Favorite period in time."

"Medieval. God, I actually got to have fun then."

Clara inhaled sharply. "The dragon legends. Those were you?"

"And my hybrid offspring at the time. Hellions, the lot of them." There was a smile in his voice, and from here, she could see his cheeks swell with a grin at the memory. "You should've seen the castles, Clara. You would've loved that entire era. Well, most of it. We glutted ourselves on ash and, for the first time, I wasn't hiding or convincing my offspring to hide. We could just be for that short period before I went into hiding again and allowed the stories of that time to fade to legend. I was too heartsick and reckless then, but damn, it felt good to let go. I took my first wife shortly after that to ground me again. I'd bred women before—humans—but I needed more than that to bring me back to my senses. I needed someone steady in my life. I didn't care for her much, but I felt protective enough to see reason behind keeping my dragon hidden."

Clara frowned and stifled the green tendrils of jealousy. He'd said he didn't care for his first wife much, so why was she feeling so possessive? He'd lived for a very long time. Of course he'd been with other women. Smoothing the frown from her face, she said, "Favorite job."

"Logger," he said, void of hesitation.

"Wait, you were a lumberjack?"

"Does that surprise you?"

She looked back in the direction of his mansion, but she couldn't see it through the trees anymore. "A little."

"I wasn't always wealthy. I've just had infinite time to figure out what works and what doesn't. I've lost my money and gone completely broke several times over taking risks with finances. You caught me after a fifty year good run is all. I've done logging several times when the money was gone. It's my fallback. The physical work settles my dragon and makes me feel almost...content. Even now, when I see the bears on their landings, when I watch them work, I miss it down to my bones."

"Why don't you work with them then if you miss it so much?"

"I hadn't ever considered it before because I was trying to keep distance between myself and the bears. It was easier not to feel anything for them if I didn't spend the extra time with the crews." Damon led her out of the woods and onto a black pebble beach. He turned and unbuttoned his jeans with a wicked grin that transformed his face.

Naughty glint in his eyes, he shucked his pants and pulled his shirt over his head, undressing completely.

"We're skinny-dipping?"

"Scared?"

"No."

"Lie."

"I've never done it before."

Damon frowned and angled his head. "I've seen your body, Clara. Your beauty steals my breath away. I love all of you. Every pattern I can trace in your freckles, the soft curve of your breasts. Your smooth skin that is only for me to touch." He reached forward and plucked a wild curl of her ruddy hair, then released it and watched it spring back into place. "I'm attracted to every single thing about you. You don't have to be shy around me."

She crinkled her nose at the surrounding woods. "It's not you that I'm worried about. What if someone sees us?"

"A modest shifter? I thought I'd seen it all.

This is private land, and no one ever comes here but me. This is my favorite place, and in all my years here, I've never seen anyone at my falls."

Okay, she felt better now. With a shy smile, she pushed her shorts and panties down and took of her shirt, but when she looked up, Damon was diving gracefully into a wave. He came out of the dark water and shook out his hair like a dog, then gave her a playful grin and jerked his chin for her to join him.

With a giddy laugh, she ran across the river beach and into the lapping waves. When she reached him, she swam past and challenged him, "I'll race you to the falls!"

She was breathless from exertion and laughter by the time she lost rather badly to Damon in a race to the pounding water and its surrounding mist cloud. In the fog, it felt more private, and she relaxed completely in his arms as he held her and swam her in slow circles until their feet touched the craggy bottom right by the waterfall. His eyes stayed trained on her as though he'd never seen anyone as beautiful.

"This is fast, isn't it?" she asked. "To feel this deeply about another person in such a short time?"

"Maybe for others. Our love story is different, though. For me, it started eons ago when I forged a connection with your ancestors. Feyadine wasn't meant for me. She was only meant to be the beginning of my journey to you. It doesn't feel fast to me."

Cheeks flushing, she pulled Damon in close and rested her chin on his shoulder. The water lapped at her in a relaxing rhythm. "I feel like I've known you my whole life."

"Haven't you though? Through your visions?"

He was right. A piece of her had always known him. Had always yearned for him. "You sure were easy to fall in love with, Dangerous Damon."

The corner of his mouth lifted against her cheek, and he angled his head just enough to rest his lips on hers and take a languid, gentle sip. "So were you, Dangerous Clara."

"Can I see him?"

"You want to see the monster inside of me?"

She angled her head and nodded. "Don't you know that's what love is? It's seeing the monster inside and staying anyway."

He shook his head and stared at her as if he couldn't believe she was in his arms right now. As if he couldn't understand how they'd gotten here. As if he was the lucky one. Silly dragon.

With a slow, clicking rumble, he steadied her on the rocky bottom and backed closer to the waterfall. His eyes blazed silver, and he hunched into himself an instant before his skin ripped open and the enormous dragon inside of him was freed. He towered over her like a building and arched his long neck high. The waterfall pounded against the sharp spikes down his back, and streams of water trailed down his scales. His head was as wide as a barn, and when he blinked, two separate eyelids closed over his eyes from the side. The snarl in his chest sounded throatier and louder now, and he moved with snake-like grace. Two long, curved spikes unfurled from the base of his head backward and were accented by smaller ones that grew in lines down his cheekbones. His armor-like scales boasted the tarnish of burns and slash marks of old battle scars, but the old injuries didn't hinder his movement as he stepped carefully through the water, arching around her, as if, even now, in the safety of the secret waterfall, he had the instinct to protect her.

He was lethal and terrifying and beautiful.

Stepping carefully over the jagged rocks beneath her bare feet, she held her palms out and made a relieved sound in her throat when her hands connected with his body. She'd expected him to be cold, but he was just as warm as he was in his human skin.

Slowly, she spread her arms out like wings and pressed her body against his. Damon's stomach rose and fell under her with his steady breath, and the slow vibration of his constant rumbling rattled her body. When he lowered his massive head, his churning silver eyes with those long, contracting pupils beheld her with something akin to pleasure.

She squeezed her eyes tightly closed and grinned as her chest filled with overwhelming joy. She'd seen him when he was blowing fire and angry, and she'd seen him like this—a gentle giant that could be so careful with her in the lapping waters of the falls.

When she opened her eyes again, the sunlight was reflecting beautifully off of his iridescent scales.

She was in this.

Clara was staying because she'd seen Damon for what he truly was.

She was staying because he was so easy to love.

With a slow smile, she whispered, "I see no monster."

ELEVEN

Damon traced the Blackwing crest on Clara's shoulder blade as softly as he was able with his fingertip.

His Clara was fast asleep in his lair. God, he'd never seen anything more beautiful. Wild, red hair curled in waves over the pillow under her cheek. Her full lips were swollen from his kisses. Her skin flushed from the heat he radiated. Her freckles stark against her fair skin, creating constellations more beautiful than the night sky. Those delicately arched ruddy eyebrows that told him every emotion she experienced.

His stunning mate didn't know it yet, but she'd wrecked him for eternity.

The first time he'd brought her into his bedroom, he'd been so scared she would find it cold, just like him, but she hadn't. She'd accepted it, just as she'd accepted him in ways that had slashed him open so wide, he would never be able to completely tuck away his emotions again.

What had she done to him, this siren? She'd bewitched him completely. She'd dispelled his fears long enough to curl into his softened heart and beg him to keep her safe and warm there, and now for the rest of her life, he would love her without abandon. It was too late for anything else. Too late to hide from her or keep his walls up. Clara had laughed at the barriers he'd erected around himself and destroyed them with a single kiss.

Some mighty dragon he was, instantly falling to pieces for the fair maiden.

Clara smiled in her sleep as he ran his finger down the ridges of her spine to the swell of her hip. He'd been with many, but none had touched what he'd just experienced with Clara. She'd been so open with him, so vulnerable, when he'd made love to her. He knew what she was. Deep down inside where she tucked the fiery grizzly that wasn't afraid of anything, she was a warrior. But with him, she let her guard down. She invited him to see the pieces of herself she'd hidden away to protect herself from the world. Against all reason, she *trusted* him. He could see it in her eyes when she'd slowed their rhythm, intertwined his fingers with hers and lifted her chin to look into his eyes as they moved toward release together.

He'd never believed in magic. A legendary shifter like him knew the truth. People looked to creatures like him to believe in something more than the black and white, but for him...there was no magic. He'd hatched and was raised in a rocky cave by his father. He blew fire because he could make gasses in his lungs when he was angry, and he'd honed the use of his firestarter. He could eat ash because that's what his animal required, and he could live forever simply because that was his chemical make-up. He was a prehistoric monster that had refused to go extinct with the rest of its kind.

No, he'd never believed in magic, but when Clara had looked up into his eyes as they'd finished with those tears of happiness streaming down the sides of her face, his way of thinking had shifted. When he'd felt that blinding sensation as the bond strengthened between them and had experienced the feeling of utter belonging with her, when he could see the make-up of her soul because his had suddenly awoken after so long being dead, for that instant, magic had existed.

He was going to love her every second for the rest of her life. And when she went gray, and her beauty faded in her own eyes, she would only become lovelier to him because he would know her time on earth was fading and his time with her even more precious.

And when she, his tragically mortal Clara, passed to the next world, he would spend eternity paying homage to her with his heart.

She would be his last mate.

She would be the only one who was real.

She would be everything.

TWELVE

The ink of Clara's tattoo moved and morphed until the ring of fire dissolved into the tiny black dragon, and the little creature moved as if the drawing was twitching to life just under her skin. Her gasp echoed loud at first, then grew softer. The drip drip of the cave wall was constant, but she couldn't see anything other than the tiny dragon who reached forward and stretched its miniature claws. There was a prickle of pain, as if the nails were needles in her flesh. Slowly, the dragon dragged itself across her skin to the tip of her collarbone, then over the slight swell of her bicep. Clara froze in fear as it circled her arm in the blink of an eye, then slowed again. It's tiny tongue flicked out of its mouth, scenting her skin, or perhaps tasting it. She wanted to rip it from her body. She wanted to claw and slash until the ink was gone, but she was helpless to move as it turned its spiked head toward her. The scent of smoke filled her nostrils, and the flash of a man's face ricocheted off her mind.

His skin was gruesome and gray, sagging as if he'd been left in the desert to dry out and die in the sun. His eyes were black and soulless, and the smile that twisted his lips was so terrifying, her gasp echoed again, though she wasn't breathing now.

"You can't hide from me, seer." His dry, cracked lips moved a moment too late to match his words.

This wasn't real. Wake up!

His face faded to reveal the dragon tattoo again, poised over the middle of her forearm.

The man's hollow voice whispered out, "We're bound, you and I."

And then the little tattooed dragon dove into the tender center of her arm. Black tendrils of ink unfurled from where it had disappeared, the darkness snaking up her arm like poison polluted streams. Pain grew brighter and harsher as the rivers of black stretched up her neck and through her chest. And just where the dragon had disappeared, in the darkest part of her body now, her skin turned to stone and cracked with the deafening sound of fault lines shifting.

Terror clogged her throat as her arm began to turn to ash, and she screamed the only name she wanted on her lips at the end. "Damon!"

Clara sat up with his name clawing its way out of her throat, and Damon was there on the bed beside her. A lantern was lit on the wall, casting a flickering candlelight glow across the worry etched into the sharp angles of his face. He had her forearm turned over in his hand, his fingertips digging deeply into her arm where he gripped it. Underneath her skin was a tiny, green light.

Damon reached behind him and pulled something from the bedside table drawer as she panted and tried to make sense of the horrifying green glow.

"Don't look," he demanded.

But she couldn't take her eyes from the light glowing beneath her skin. The flick of a knife blade was loud and clashed against the gentle dripping of the cave wall behind them. Before she had time to jerk away, he cut a skilled slit into her arm and dug something out of her arm.

Pain registered an instant later, but he already had the thing in his palm and was rushing away from her.

"Fuck!" he yelled, hunching into himself and flinging his hand. Something thick and sticky lobbed from his fingertips and made a splat sound against the stone floor.

Clara gasped out, "Oh, my gosh," as the spatters of liquid caught fire around the edges and burned through the stone until she couldn't see them anymore.

Damon clutched his hand to his middle and snarled out a pained sound.

Clara bolted for him. "Let me see it."

"No," he growled, shaking his head hard. "It's best if you don't."

"Let me see it, Damon!"

Damon's shoulders heaved with his panting breath as he stared at her, but at last, he slowly unclenched his fist from his middle and exposed his palm. Clara's heart sank to her toes, and her eyes burned with tears. "Oh, love."

His skin was mangled and raw. There wasn't any blood to get in the way of his exposed meat, as if the gel in that capsule had burned him so quickly, it had cauterized his veins. There was no skin left to cover his exposed musculature.

Where he'd cut that thing out of her arm,

she was already healing and the blood easily wiped away, but Damon's hand was repairing itself much slower, just along the edges of the injury. The pain must be excruciating.

"You saved me from that...that...what was that? How did it get in my arm?"

Damon blinked slowly, and the change in his eyes was instant. Shock turned to dark comprehension. "It was put in there a long time ago, Clara, when you weren't paying attention or perhaps when you weren't conscious."

"By who?"

"By someone who'd planned your death for a very long time. By someone who has planned my torture accordingly."

"I don't understand. Is it acid? Why would anyone want to kill me?"

"It's not acid, no." He looked down at his ruined hand and sighed. "This is the work of the chemical equivalent of dragon's fire. Impossible to make unless you have the real thing on hand to start with."

"Damon," she whispered brokenly. "What's happening?"

Damon dragged his blazing, inhuman gaze to hers. "I'm not the last immortal dragon after all."

Clara couldn't catch her breath. It felt as if someone was standing on her chest, forcing all the air from her. "Marcus," she whispered. "My dream. Black eyes, skin sloughed off. Not like your scars. Worse. He said I can't hide from him." God, why couldn't she breathe? That capsule of dragon's fire had been meant for her. Meant to kill her, but Damon had taken the pain out of her and onto himself to protect her.

Tears streamed down her face as he clenched his hand and hid the injury from her again. More protection. She snatched the robe from the end of the bed. "I'm going to get help."

"Clara, there's nothing anyone can do."

"I'll be back," she called behind her as she bolted across the cold stones toward the door, pulling the soft robe around her shoulders as she ran.

She couldn't just stand there while her mate's body tried to repair itself from something so horrific. She couldn't just watch the pain in his eyes and not try to help. She loved him. Damon's pain was her pain.

Mason would know what to do.

Her robe flapped around her legs as she sprinted down the hallway toward the stairwell. There was an elevator that would take her to Mason's wing on the next floor, but damned if she was going to wait as the small cage carried her slowly upward. No, right now, she needed to run. She took the curving stairs two at a time, heart pounding as she screamed, "Mason!"

Reaching for the double door handles of his bedroom, she screamed at the same moment he flung open the door, dark hair disheveled and nothing but a pair of navy plaid boxers clinging to his hips. "What's happened?"

"It's Damon! He—"

"Where?" he demanded.

"His bedroom."

Mason pushed past her and flew down the stairs so fast she struggled to keep up. "I had a dream about something awful in my arm, and when I woke up, my arm was glowing."

"Glowing?"

"Yeah, glowing green. It was a capsule of something that had turned on. It was like it was preparing to detonate. Damon cut it out of my arm, but it ruptured in his hand, and he said it was like dragon's fire."

"How'd it get in your arm, Clara?" he called over his shoulder as he jumped over the last three stairs and ran toward Damon's room.

"I don't know."

Mason spun and gripped her shoulders so hard, she swore his fingers hit bone. "Who the fuck put it in you?"

"Marcus," she said on a breath.

Mason yanked his hands away as if she'd burned him. "What?"

Now the tears were back, blurring her vision as she rushed out, "Mason, I don't know how he put it in my arm. I don't remember it ever hurting or—"

"Swear to me you didn't do this, Clara. Swear it!"

"I swear I had nothing to do with hurting him, Mason! I never would! I love him! I love him more than my own fucking life. He's the air—" Her voice cracked, so she swallowed hard and continued in a ragged whisper. "He's the air I breathe. I don't know how Marcus did it. I have no memory of it."

A long, low rumble sounded from the other side of Damon's bedroom doors, and Mason gave her one last questioning look before his gaze fell to her bare feet. He turned his head, exposing his neck. "I beg your apology. He's my best friend."

"I understand," she said, her voice nothing

more than a wisp of air with her throat so tight. "You care for him, too. You're the first person I thought of when I wanted to get him help. Please help him."

Mason nodded once and strode into Damon's room. Clara followed.

Damon was sitting on the edge of his bed, hand clenched in his lap and a dangerous growl emanating from his chest. His eyes looked like swirling mercury, and his long pupils were so contracted, they were nothing but slivers of dark in all of that brilliant color. Her bear begged her to run from the power that emanated from him. Her skin prickled with the urge to defend herself, but Damon wasn't posing any threat to her. He was sitting on the bed, his focus on Mason.

His lip twitched, and he tilted his chin upward as Mason approached with his head lowered and his gaze on the ground. "She's forgiven me. I misspoke. Please, may I see it?"

Silence descended on the room for the span of three slow breaths, and then Damon nodded his head once and offered his palm, unfurling his fingers slowly from the mangled flesh. It was still open and raw. Skinless. The pain he'd shown her earlier was no longer there. He'd gone cold again, and his eyes hollow.

Clara looked away to save her insides from being shredded. The empty look didn't belong on her warm dragon's face.

Mason studied it carefully and murmured a curse. "I need to call Diem."

"I'll call her," Clara rushed out, desperate for a way to help.

"Tell her what's happened and ask if Danielle has anything made up for burns. And I need water and clean cloths. Lots of them."

"Okay," she huffed out, relieved for a job to do. After snatching her phone off the nightstand, she ran back down the hall toward the kitchen and dialed the number off the *it was so nice to meet you* text Diem had sent her after they'd met.

"Hello?" Diem asked on the second ring. Sleep filled her voice.

"Diem, it's Clara. It's late, and I'm so sorry for calling you right now, but your father has been burned badly by dragon's fire, and Mason said Danielle might have something made up for it."

"Dragon's fire? What do you mean? No, no time. Explain it to me when I get there. I'll wake Danielle. If she doesn't have anything made up, I'll help her. I'll text you on how long it will be. Clara?"

"Yeah?"

"Are you okay?"

"Yes." Clara slowed and slammed her shoulder blades against the wall as a wave of emotion took her. "I almost wasn't. Damon saved me. He protected me."

Diem let off a stressed out sigh and said, "Clara, I'll be there as soon as I can to help."

"Thank you," she squeaked out right before the call ended.

Thank God for Mason and Diem being so close. Clara was in over her head and had no idea what to do for Damon, but he'd built a family and friends around him who could help. With a sniffle, Clara wiped her damp lashes with her shaking knuckles and made her way into the kitchen. Supplies gathered, she bolted for Damon's room as fast as the giant bowl of water allowed without sloshing out the sides. When she returned, Mason had been banished to a corner chair, and Damon was pacing in front of the window panels he'd opened. Outside, the starry sky stretched on forever. The forest in front of them was bathed in hues of purple under the half moon.

"I don't understand why he's waited all this time," Mason murmured.

"Because he was waiting for her," Damon gritted out, more growl than words. "He's been waiting for Feyadine's line to produce a doppelganger. And not just any doppelganger. There could have been tens of them, but I wasn't interested. He could've put a kill switch in all of them for all we know. From birth! All he needed for me to do was to find her, so he could rip her away. And he almost succeeded!" he yelled in a booming voice. "I could've lost her!" Damon spun around, and his gaze collided with Clara's. His voice dipped lower. "I could've lost you. If I wasn't sleeping right beside you—"

"But you were, and I'm okay because of you."

Damon shook his head, back and forth, back and forth, and something flashed through his eyes for just a moment before it was replaced by fury again. Fear?

"You don't understand," he whispered. "When I lose you, it will be the middle ages all over again. The earth will burn, and I won't be able to stop myself. It's the only way my dragon knows how to mourn."

"Damon," she said on a breath.

"Dangerous Clara," he said. "You weren't ever just a danger to me." He gestured toward the open window with his good hand. "You were a danger to them as well. I'm not ready to lose you." His dark eyebrow arched, and his voice turned to steel. "I won't."

She believed him.

Oh, Marcus was coming, and he was going to bring hell with him.

Her intended death by dragon's fire was meant to let Damon know he was still alive.

Running was pointless.

Hiding wouldn't work.

But if the death-bringer look in her mate's eyes was anything to go by, Marcus had just called Damon's animal to war.

And if Damon failed to rid the world of Marcus once and for all, it didn't matter whether Clara lived or died.

The earth would burn anyway.

THIRTEEN

A booming knock sounded down the hallway. Clara looked up from the floor outside Damon's office where she'd been throwing tarot cards and frowned, waiting. Mason was in the office with Damon, but would get it, surely. He got frustrated if she stepped on his duties, so she'd learned to just let him do his running-of-the-household gig and steer clear.

With a sigh, she looked back down at the three cards she'd just drawn for Damon. He hadn't shuffled them like she usually did with paying clients, but she'd perched outside the office he was working in and focused on him when she'd shuffled and cut the deck into three piles.

She'd drawn for his past, present, and future twice, just to make sure, and for the first time since she'd been doing tarot card readings, she'd drawn the exact same card twice.

For his past, 8 of Cups made sense. He had chosen to live in a situation that hadn't worked for him. Perhaps he hadn't chosen immortality, but it had been his choice to harden his heart to everyone to protect himself.

For his present, the card she'd drawn also made sense. The Hanged Man. His life was at a crossroads, and there was something he needed to let go of. *Cough, cough, Feyadine's paintings.*

But twice now, she'd drawn a card for his future that made the blood drain from her face and limbs. A black armored rider atop a pure white horse with a woman turned away, and a child offering him a bouquet of wilted flowers.

Death.

Now, Death rarely actually meant that someone would die, and more often indicated the need to be open to change. It was more of a transformation card. But pulling it twice in a row on Damon's future had her hair standing on end.

The resounding knock reverberated down the marble hallway again, so she scooped up the cards, shoved them into her back pocket to think about later, and jogged toward the front entrance. "I'm coming!" But before she pulled open the door, she wised up and asked, "Who is it?" Because she sure as hell wasn't dumb enough to just open the front door for Fuck Face Marcus.

"It's Creed and the other alphas, here to meet with Damon at his request."

With a grunt for her efforts, Clara pulled a giant potted plant across the floor, and in front of the door stood on the pot and stared out the stupidly tall peephole. Sure enough, five men stood outside, and two of them she'd met before.

When she finally pulled the heavy doors open, they greeted her with somber smiles and Creed introduced her to the striking blue-eyed alpha of the Ashe Crew, Tagan, and the dark-haired alpha of the Boarlanders, Harrison, and lastly to a giant of a man with shoulders as wide as a redwood. His dark eyes crinkled as he offered his hand for a shake. "I'm Kong of the Gray Backs and the Lowlanders."

"Kong?" she asked through a grin as she shook his hand. He just about rattled her bones. "You don't smell like a bear, King

Kong."

"Gorilla shifter," he said with a nod, confirming her suspicion.

Oh, she bet he was a beast when he Changed. "You're the first gorilla shifter I've met," she announced. "Damon is straight down that hallway on the left. He and Mason are in the office."

Creed gave her a sideways hug as the others stepped into Damon's house. "How are you holding up?"

Apparently word spread quickly when anything dramatic happened in these mountains. "I'm okay. Just worried about Damon."

"Your mate?" he asked low.

Heat flushed her cheeks, and she hugged his side tightly and nodded. "My mate."

"Glad to hear it, Grandma."

"Eee, I hadn't thought about that. Ha! I would be your…step-grandma? Weird. I'll be sure to send you birthday cards with five dollar bills in them."

Creed pumped his fist and hissed, "Yes."

With a laugh, she swatted his arm and told him, "Go to your meeting before Damon eats you."

Her chest rose and fell deeply as she

watched the four alphas saunter down the hallway. Tagan made sure to splash Creed with the fountain water that spewed from the naked Grecian man's penis as they passed.

Clara turned to the final visitor, who lingered at the threshold. "Hi Beaston."

He ducked his head respectfully. "Mate of the Dragon."

The title brushed over her skin, lifting gooseflesh in its wake. "Do you want to come in?"

"In there?" he asked, his dark eyebrows jacked up and his eyes blazing an inhuman seafoam green. "Fuck no. Too many ghosts."

Clara turned and narrowed her eyes at the shadowy figures who lined the hallway. Honestly, she'd gotten used to their presence as she imagined Damon had gotten used to them over the centuries. That or Damon couldn't see them. But apparently, Beaston could.

"You see beyond the veil, too?"

He backed away from the door. "Like my Mom did. I have a gift for you."

She stepped out the door and shut the huge wooden barriers behind her. Then she sat beside Beaston on the porch stair.

"I was going to wrap it pretty, the way girls

like. Glittery paper and ribbon and fancy shit, but I need to tell you why I'm giving you this, and I don't write good."

"Okay."

He pulled a long knife from his belt, the blade gleaming in the sunlight. "I've made knives for all my Gray Back girls, and I know you like things that match." Beaston swallowed hard and shook his head as he handed it to her, hilt first. "I wanted to make it small like theirs, but you have a big job to do."

"What kind of job?"

"I had a dream."

"About me?" she asked, her voice nothing but a shocked squeak.

"No," he murmured, leveling her with his wild eyes. "About her. About your job."

"Her?"

"He's going to ask you to leave, Clara. Don't go. Stay here. Fight. Fight even if you think it's over. Fight until you're dead. Fight until she's dead."

Clara stared down at the long, sharp blade of the knife in her open palms. He'd etched her tattoo into the silver near the handle and had carved *D + C* along the curve of the dragon's spine.

"Damon and Clara?" she whispered.

Beaston nodded and ran his thumb under her eye. He frowned at the drop of moisture on the pad. "Soft bear. Soft and full of tears. So soft you'll bring our dragon to his knees." He lifted that inhuman gaze back to her. "Save him."

Beaston stood and strode for a tree where a shiny, feathered raven sat on the lowest branch.

"Save him?" she called.

Beaston didn't turn around or answer. He simply held his forearm out for his Aviana to wrap her small talons around, and then he disappeared into the woods with his mate.

How could she save Damon from Marcus? How could she save anyone? She was a sometimes-defective clairvoyant grizzly shifter—not a fire-breathing dragon.

Clara felt completely helpless to fight against the force that was coming, but Beaston had given her a twelve-inch blade and told her to do just that.

She wiped her still damp lashes on her shoulder and picked up the fine leather sheath that sat in the exact place Beaston had. After sliding the blade safely inside, she clutched it to her chest and stared at the place the half-wild bear shifter had disappeared.

She'd felt a connection to the man from the first time she'd met him at the barbecue with the Gray Backs, but maybe her intuition of his brokenness didn't lie.

Perhaps Beaston really was crazy.

FOURTEEN

"Have you seen him?" Clara asked Mason, who sat at the kitchen island, sipping a mug of steaming coffee.

Damon hadn't been in bed when she'd woken up an hour ago, and he hadn't shown up while she was readying for the day. And after searching all his favorite haunts in the house, he was still a no show.

"He's out on the terrace."

"There's a terrace?"

Mason chuckled and stood. He made a second cup of coffee and handed it to her. "I wanted to say something to you."

"Oh God, what did I do now?"

He laughed, and a blanket of relief slid over her shoulders. She wasn't in trouble then.

"You've done nothing but good. Listen, I know you didn't like me much for bringing you up here on false pretenses, and I wish I had a good excuse why I did it. All I can say is that you felt important. I went back to your file over and over for the last year, and I got chills every time I read it. And I want to say I'm sorry, but I also want to say I don't regret what I did." Mason canted his head and murmured, "You brought him back to life, Clara."

She took the offered mug of fragrant coffee from his hands and leaned onto the island. "I was really mad at you at first, but I already forgave you days ago. You brought me to Damon. You brought me to these mountains." She shrugged. "I get chills here a lot, too. The good kind. The kind where I feel like I am right where I'm supposed to be. So I guess what I'm saying is I'm glad you brought me here, and I'm glad you've been there for Damon. He's lucky to have a friend like you."

"We should come up with a crew name," Mason teased.

Clara snorted. "It needs to be badass."

"I'll get right on that."

"A pig, a bear, and a dragon walk into a bar..."

"Don't finish that joke," Mason said, stifling a smile.

"The Pork Rind Crew."

"I'll take you to the terrace now."

And he did. Mason led her down past Damon's bedroom, down the dark halls with the old fashioned lanterns, down a narrow walkway surrounded by rock walls, and through a set of dark double doors to an opening in the cliffs. There were no windows separating the smooth rock floor from the woods below. And standing on the edge was Damon, a striking silhouette in his dark suit with his hands on his hips as he looked over his domain. He'd removed the bandages from his right hand, and from here, it already looked half healed, though scarred. More scars, and how many would his body bear before this was through?

Mason squeezed her shoulder and left her there.

The wind whistled through the opening, hard enough that it would likely blow her over if she got too close to the ledge, but Damon stood as if the wind did not affect him. As if he was part of the stone here. She couldn't even tell if he was breathing.

"You weren't in bed when I woke up."

"Were you worried?" he asked softly, though his voice sounded like gravel and was punctuated with a long rumble.

"A little," she admitted. He'd drawn into himself over the last week, and she hated that he was pushing her away. "I worry about losing you."

"You won't."

"No, I mean, I'm worried you'll push me away."

Damon turned slowly, his eyes glowing silver in the shadows of the cave terrace. "I…" He blinked slowly and turned his back on her again. "I think you should leave."

"I'm not going anywhere."

"It's not safe for you here—"

"It's not safe for me out there! Damon, you tried hiding your people before and it didn't save them. It didn't protect them. I'm staying here, with you." Clara touched the knife on her belt just to reassure herself. She wore it everywhere now. "I understand why you sent the crews away. I do. But I'm not part of their crews, Damon. I'm part of yours. Don't send me away."

He huffed a single, humorless laugh. "I knew you'd refuse."

She approached slowly, wrapped her arms around his middle, and rested her cheek right between his shoulder blades. "Then why did you even ask?"

"Because I had to try, Clara." His hand slid up her forearm and rested against her hands, keeping her touch there, just over his heart. His voice rang hollow when he murmured, "This place feels empty without them."

She understood. He'd grown to care for the crews. The Ashe Crew and the Boarlanders. The Gray Backs and Kong's Lowlanders. They had become a part of Damon's mountains just as surely as the trees and forest animals.

"When this is all through, they'll be back." She hoped so because the pain and loneliness in Damon's voice had cracked her heart open.

"And what if it's never over? What if Marcus waits for years to come for me? To come for you? I'll miss their entire lives. I'll miss the babies growing up." Damon swallowed audibly and squeezed her hands as if her letting go right now would hurt him.

Shadows danced across the walls in the glow of the lanterns, and Clara cast them a frown. Restless ghosts, uncomfortable with this kind of talk.

Damon turned in her arms, and his lips crashed onto hers. These weren't the sweet kisses he used to tell her wordlessly that he loved her. This was allowing her to see the pain he was in. His lips were unforgiving as he deepened the kiss and thrust his tongue into her mouth. He let off a helpless sound and walked her backward. She gasped as her back hit the cold cave wall. Wrapping her arms around his neck, she bit his bottom lip and kissed him back so he could see how scared she was. He should see how determined she was to stay by his side despite that fear.

Something brushed her neck. A soft mist, like a tendril of fog, skittered across her skin, lifting gooseflesh. Clara jumped and pulled her mouth from Damon's.

"What's wrong?" he asked.

Clara stood frozen against him, breathing heavily as something sat just above her senses. A vibration out of place, or a change in the wind. She looked to the lantern shadows on her left, and the shadowy figures that had been so restless before were melting into the walls. Damon followed her gaze as another tendril of air curled over her shoulder.

"Clara, what are they saying?"

There was a soft whisper of something. A word. So soft, she had to strain her sensitive ears. Fear pounded through her veins as she lifted her horrified gaze to Damon.

"Your ghosts are telling us to run."

A shadow covered the mouth of the

opening, blocking out the sun, and Clara screamed as the massive head of a black dragon reached its long neck into the cave and opened his mouth. Rows of razor sharp teeth reached for them as the first clicks of a Firestarter echoed through the cliff opening.

"Go!" Damon yelled, shoving her toward the hallway.

Time slowed. Damon ran behind her, shoving her forward and shielding her with his back. She pushed her legs as hard as she could and screamed as heat blasted from behind them.

"Faster," Damon ordered. "Don't look back."

Flames filled the hallway just inches behind them and coming fast. She ran for her life. She ran for Damon's life because every instinct in her body screamed that he would never leave her to save himself.

Mason was there, waiting at the double doors. "Hurry!"

Clara's legs burned and gave out the second she passed through, and she watched in horror as Damon turned and helped Mason close the doors against the fire. Flames licked through the cracks, and Mason gritted his teeth in pain as the metal decorated bands on the door heated and turned red against his hands.

Clara looked down at her body. It was betraying her. The inner grizzly she'd always been able to rely on when she was scared was curled up in a ball in her middle, and her arms and legs were tingling as if they'd fallen asleep.

Damon slammed down a wooden bar over the door and yanked her up, then hauled her down the hallway to his bedroom. "I have to get to open air. It's too tight to Change in here."

But just as he turned the corner to his bedroom door, the sound of shattering glass turned deafening.

Another scream lodged in Clara's throat as she got a glimpse of Marcus's long onyx-colored claws raking across the bedroom, destroying everything. A stream of fire and magma spewed through the room an instant after Damon and Mason had dragged her across the open doorway.

Work legs! She felt as if she were floating. As if her body wasn't under her control anymore.

They missed fire by inches as the monster followed them room to room, clinging to the outside of the house, destroying it in his quest to get to them. The white marble hallway was the last barrier between them and air, but the fire was too close behind them, following them, singeing Clara's skin. Where was her fucking bear?

No good. The hallway stretched on and on, and they weren't moving fast enough to escape the flames blasting around them.

"Damon!" she screamed just as the fire reached her back because, dammit, this was the tragedy. One week with him. One week of happiness. One week of feeling like she finally, finally belonged somewhere, and she was dying by dragon's fire with the two men who'd become her crew.

"Hold on!" Damon ordered as he scooped her and Mason by the waist.

Power pulsed against her, stealing her breath as Damon's battle cry turned into a bellowing roar. The space was too tight for him to Change, but that didn't stop the enormous blue dragon that burst from his skin. Tucking them tight to his stomach with oversize claws, he exploded from the mansion and drove his powerful wings against the air, lifting them as the house shattered behind them. Marcus's flames blasted around Damon's exposed back as he shielded her and

Mason and dropped them low to the ground. The drop was still too high. She and Mason tumbled end over end and Clara screamed out in pain as she slammed into a tree, arm first.

Struggling to her feet, she ducked as Damon collided with Marcus against the side of the destroyed house, blasting glass like bullets across the clearing. Clara held up her arm to shield her face as pain slashed across her skin. Mason yanked her backward a moment too late and hugged her tight as dragon's fire filled the air. The roar of the battling dragons rattled her head and made her dizzy, and still, her bear was buried too deep to reach.

Mason was yelling something she couldn't understand. Yelling. Yelling. *I don't understand!* She couldn't take her eyes off the warring dragons as they beat their wings against the air and lifted off the ground, clinging to each other's claws as they blew streams of flaming lava.

Searing pain rocketed up the nerve endings in her arm as Mason jerked a broken bone into place. "Fuck!" she screamed in shock. A power she didn't understand pulsed from her body and blew Mason twenty yards away. He landed on all fours and slid backward through the dirt before he came to a stop, eyes locked on hers.

"Oh, my God," she whispered, looking at her tingling palms. The lines on her hands were glowing orange, and now when she tried to close her fists, she wasn't in control of her body enough to do so

Let me in. The words whispered across her mind. *Let me save him.*

What the hell was happening to her?

A slash of pain built just behind her eyes in the same headache she'd been fighting off and on her entire life. This time it was different though. This time it didn't throb or fade away. It grew and grew, brighter and more agonizing until she was nothing at all.

Mason was on his knees in the dirt, bleeding from a hundred places where the glass had damaged him and staring at her with blazing blue, inhuman eyes as if he'd never seen her before. "Feyadine?"

Chills blasted up her body with the rightness of that name. *I'm here.*

"Change, Mason. I'll need you." She flicked her fingertips at Mason, and a massive, black boar with long, curved tusks and blazing, furious eyes burst from his body. He was as tall as her, much bigger than any wild boar.

Coarse, long fur spiked up over his powerful back, raised with his fury, and as he lifted his attention to the sky, he dragged a massive hoof through the dirt, ready for battle. All this time, Mason had been hiding a monster inside of him, too.

She dragged her gaze back to the warring dragons above. She clenched her hands at her sides as waves of light pulsed from her body upward until it reached the clouds. Above her, the early morning sunshine disappeared as dark clouds drew around them, flashing jagged bolts of lightning time and time again. Ash from the dragon fire rained down over everything as Damon fought for his life. As he fought for hers. As he fought to keep the world safe from the reign of death and destruction Marcus would bring if there was no force able to oppose him anymore. He'd waited a very long time to build enough strength to carry out his vengeance on Damon. Was Clara's death a part of his plan to weaken Damon? Was she a distraction he'd carefully aimed at the last Bloodrunner dragon? It was just like black-hearted Marcus to use love as a weapon.

The dragons were above the clouds now, nothing but flashes of orange above the gray.

Red fury filled her veins with purpose as

she screamed and slammed her hands down onto the ground. The earth cracked under her touch, and a towering spray of steam shot up to open space in the clouds. There they were. The dragons who had caused her to wait for eons for this moment. One had driven her with hate, one with love, and today, as the last thing she ever did on this earth, she would right the wrongs done by Marcus's evil.

Gritting her teeth, she thrust her palms upward, one at each dragon. Streams of power reached them, and she pulled them apart. With Markus roaring his fury, she slammed her fist into the ground, and the black dragon tumbled to earth and smashed against the surface, cracking the ground beneath her feet with the impact. The earthquake that followed rattled her to her bones, but she held her focus and lowered Damon slowly.

Everything made sense as she forced Marcus to Change back into his hideous human form.

Save him. Beaston's voice brushed across her mind.

I'll find you again, and when I do, I'll be stronger. I'll gift you mortality with the blood of an immortal dragon, and you'll be free. She'd uttered those words all those centuries ago, and today was the day of reckoning. Today, she would follow through for the last Bloodrunner dragon.

I'll find you again. She'd found him through Clara and had fed off his love to be strong enough for this.

God, let her be strong enough.

She slid Beaston's knife from its sheath at her hip and held it steady at her side as she strode toward Marcus. Her bare feet made footprints in the blanket of ash, and it fell like snow in front of her as Marcus stood to his full human height. Burns covered his body, and he smelled of burned flesh.

His demon-black eyes narrowed with hatred. "You bitch. What have you done to me?"

She offered him an empty smile. "I took your dragon away. Payback for you killing me."

"Obviously, Clara, I did not kill you. Not for lack of trying, though. I've put capsules of fire into every one of Nall's red-headed descendants, just waiting for Damon to choose one of you. How could he not? You all looked the same. Exactly his type. Don't worry, though. I'll finish you off once I'm done with your mate."

"You killed me and ripped my eggs from my womb!" she screamed.

Marcus's face fell slack and his eyes went wide as he took a step back. "Feyadine?" He shook his head. "No, it's impossible."

His putrid face sagged like clay, and she reveled in the change in his features. He'd been a handsome dragon warrior once, but Damon had done this to him. Damon had burned him to avenge her and the rest of the dragons he'd murdered in cold blood. Pride surged through her as she whispered, "Do you remember the incantation you did on the ceremonial knife you used to cut me open? The one that allowed you to cut my skin so easily?"

Marcus backed up another step and shook his head, and the scent of bitter fear wafted from his skin.

"I do," she murmured low, stalking him step for step.

"You're just a seer."

"No," Feyadine said with a dark chuckle. "You were wrong about so much. I was never a seer, Marcus. I was a witch." She murmured the incantation over Beaston's blade, just a whisper of words so ancient and so dark, they tasted like poison on her tongue. The blade glowed orange, so bright, it was hard to look at. She clenched her fist, freezing Marcus's body into place as she strode up to him and ran the blade over his stomach until black blood oozed from his skin and coated the knife, sizzling as it settled into the engraving Beaston had done of the Blackwing crest.

A wave of dizziness took her, and she stumbled forward, breath ragged as her power waned. *Hold on just a minute longer. Finish this.*

Marcus looked down defiantly at her, frozen under her will. "You meddling bitch. You can't kill me, Feyadine. We're bound. Now let me Change into my dragon so I can finish this."

Her lip twitched as a branch snapped in the woods surrounding them. Feyadine backed up a few steps with the knowledge he was right. He'd done awful things to her when she'd been his so many lifetimes ago. He'd bound them. He'd made it so she could never kill him.

But she didn't need to.

She spun in a slow circle. The woods were alive with towering, snarling grizzlies of every color. Two silverback gorillas beat their chest like war drums and pulled their lips back to expose long, razor sharp canines. Mason's monstrous boar lowered his head and trotted closer, blood lust in his feral eyes. A falcon and a raven circled overhead, crying out a death chant, and clinging to the cliffs above was Diem's green and gold dragon. Feyadine's eyes stung with emotion as her gaze landed on Damon, Changed back into his human form. He was badly burned down one side, and his chest was heaving as he saw the same thing she did.

His crews had never left him as he'd asked.

They'd come for him just like he'd always been there for them.

The Ashe Crew, Boarlanders, Gray Backs, and Lowlanders had gathered together, ready to come help Damon finish this.

"I don't need to kill you, Marcus. You thought Damon caring for others made him weak, but you were wrong. And now you're at the end of your life, and you'll spend your last breath as you deserve. Alone."

Beaston stepped through a line of grizzlies, eyes blazing inhuman green over his empty smile. "Can we kill him now?"

Feyadine dragged her glare to Marcus. She'd never seen fear in his eyes before, but there it was now.

She stood back and nodded her chin once. A massive silver grizzly burst from Beaston and roared as he led the charge. The inhabitants of Damon's mountains bore down on Marcus from all sides, and he screamed a doomed sound as he disappeared in the middle of teeth and claws.

Feyadine stumbled backward, arms tingling with weakness. *Stay strong. Finish this. Damon's love for Clara is infinite. It has to be to give me this much power. Clara is good. So much better than me. He deserves to grow old with his Clara.*

"I'm sorry," she murmured as she reached Damon and jerked his palm up. She ran the bloody, glowing blade across his skin, and she winced as the final pulse of power left her body.

Damon stared down at the blood that poured freely from the slice across his hand with eyes gone round.

She fell as all of the strength left her body, and Damon cradled her against his chest before she hit the ground. Looking up into those silver eyes, the ones that she'd fallen in love with once upon a time, she uttered the oath she'd made to him all those centuries ago, "You won't be alone anymore. I found you again, and when I did, I was stronger. I gifted you mortality with the blood of an immortal dragon." She gasped as she left Clara's body, and on her last breath, she whispered, "Now, you're free."

FIFTEEN

Clara's hands wouldn't stop trembling as she rocked in one of the chairs on the sprawling porch of the old trailer in the Grayland Mobile Park. Damon and the Gray Backs would be home any moment now, and she had some big news that made her feel giddy and faint all at the same time.

So much had changed since Marcus's death. Clara had fallen unconscious for two days after Feyadine had left her body, and when she woke up, her world had been turned on its axis. She remembered everything Feyadine had done through her. And now, Feyadine's presence was gone from her life completely, taking the headaches, nightmares, and memories with her.

Damon's house had been demolished to nothing but a pile of rubble and glass. She'd been so scared that he would be heartbroken, but he hadn't seemed to care one bit, and moving into the old singlewide trailer, 1010, in the Gray Back's trailer park had been a seamless transition. Even Mason had taken up residence in Clinton's abandoned trailer.

Perhaps Damon would rebuild his house at the top of his mountains, or perhaps they would live here for always, she didn't know. But by God, it did her soul good to watch her mate thrive here.

Even in this old trailer, so different from his sprawling cliff mansion, he smiled constantly and filled their tiny house with the sound of his laughter.

She hadn't ever imagined she could be this happy.

The sound of the trucks coming down the mountain switchbacks from the landing above perked her sensitive ears right up. Willa, Aviana, Georgia, and Gia came from the direction of the worm farm out back and stood by the bricked in fire-pit, waiting on their mates to return from a long day cutting lumber, as Clara waited for hers.

Damon was a logger again. He didn't do it for the money. He did this job with the bears who had become a family to him because it made him happy. Because he was allowing himself to get close to the people he cared about now, instead of hiding away in his tower, protecting his heart.

As the lead truck came around the bend in the white gravel road, Willa whistled and called out, "A-team!"

With a laugh, Clara stood from her rocking chair and locked her arms against the porch railing as her heart rate kicked up to a gallop. Her Damon was almost home.

The procession of trucks was short, thanks to the boys riding together in the mornings. Damon slid out of the passenger's seat of Creed's gunmetal gray jacked-up Ford pickup and nodded his goodbye to the guys as they piled out. When his dark eyes locked on hers, she froze at how strikingly handsome he was.

He'd admitted that he'd worn the suits to hide the burn scars on his arms, but no more. A dirt-smeared white T-shirt clung to his muscular shoulders, and his jeans were frayed and had holes at the knees. His dark hair was mussed from being under a hardhat, and his shoes were no longer the polished loafers he used to wear. Instead, they were mud splattered work-boots. And damn, that bright smile nearly knocked her feet out from under her.

She mirrored his happiness with an answering smile and jogged down the porch stairs to meet him. He dropped his lunch pail and scooped her up, kissing her as if he hadn't seen her in weeks. This right here, this moment, was her favorite part of every day.

Easing back, she rested her forearms on his shoulders and looked happily down at him. "I have a surprise for you."

"Oh yeah?" He quirked his lips. "Is it meatloaf?"

Clara laughed and squirmed as he tickled her ribs. Swatting him, she muttered, "I'm serious, and no it's not my famously bad meatloaf." Leaning forward, she whispered into his ear, "I figured out why I haven't been able to Change into my bear."

Damon's arms went rigid around her backside. "Why?" he asked on a breath.

"Because we're going to have a baby."

Damon buried his face against her neck as his breathing went uneven. "Love, tell me it's true. Tell me."

"I took a dozen pregnancy tests. All positive." She nuzzled her cheek against his hair. "Are you happy?"

Damon bit her collarbone playfully and

eased back, stunning her with the emotion that pooled in his eyes.

"Happiness isn't a big enough word. You've given me so much, Clara. Your heart, my mortality, and now this? A child?" He settled her on the ground and stood back, gripping her hips and staring down at her stomach. He sighed and shook his head, as if he couldn't believe how lucky he'd gotten.

He didn't see what she did, though. She had lucked into a life she hadn't even dreamed of, and it was all because of him. Damon had saved her in so many ways, and now he'd given her this gift. He'd given her a child. He'd given her the chance to be a mate and a mother. He'd given her his unconditional love.

Her heart was so full, it was hard to speak. Forcing words past her tightening chest, she whispered, "We'll get to raise our baby here in your mountains. Our child can protect your treasure when we're gone."

"Don't you see it, Clara?" Damon murmured, lifting that beautiful, silver gaze to hers. "The mountains aren't my treasure anymore." His smile was slow and adoring as he brushed his thumbs over her stomach. "You are."

Want More of These Characters?

Try T. S. Joyce's Bestselling
Gray Back Bears Series.

The Complete Series is Available Now

Gray Back Bad Bear
(Gray Back Bears, Book 1)

About the Author

T.S. Joyce is devoted to bringing hot shifter romances to readers. Hungry alpha males are her calling card, and the wilder the men, the more she'll make them pour their hearts out. She werebear swears there'll be no swooning heroines in her books. It takes tough-as-nails women to handle her shifters.

Experienced at handling an alpha male of her own, she lives in a tiny town, outside of a tiny city, and devotes her life to writing big stories. Foodie, wolf whisperer, ninja, thief of tiny bottles of awesome smelling hotel shampoo, nap connoisseur, movie fanatic, and zombie slayer, and most of this bio is true.

Bear Shifters? Check
Smoldering Alpha Hotness? Double Check
Sexy Scenes? Fasten up your girdles, ladies and gents, it's gonna to be a wild ride.

For more information on T. S. Joyce's work,
visit her website at
www.tsjoycewrites.wordpress.com

Made in United States
Orlando, FL
03 May 2023

32742248R00114